Emily Windsnap and the Castle in the Mist

LIZ KESSLER

illustrations by NATACHA LEDWIDGE

CANDLEWICK PRESS
CAMBRIDGE, MASSACHUSETTS

Text copyright © 2007 by Liz Kessler
Illustrations copyright © 2007 by Natacha Ledwidge

First published in Great Britain in 2007
by Orion Children's Books,
a division of the Orion Publishing Group

Published by arrangement with Orion Children's Books

First U.S. edition 2007

Library of Congress Cataloging-in-Publication Data
Kessler, Emily.
Emily Windsnap and the castle in the mist / Liz Kessler ; illustrated by Natacha Ledwidge. —1st U.S. ed.
p. cm.
Summary: When she incurs Neptune's wrath by finding a diamond ring buried under rocks in the ocean, Emily is put under a curse that will force her to choose to be either a mermaid or a human and split up her parents forever.
ISBN 978-0-7636-3330-1
[1. Mermaids—Fiction. 2. Rings—Fiction. 3. Blessing and cursing—Fiction. 4. Friendship—Fiction. 5. Neptune (Roman deity)—Fiction.]
I. Ledwidge, Natacha, ill. II. Title. III. Title: Castle in the mist.
PZ7.K4842Emc 2007
[Fic]—dc22   2006051835

2 4 6 8 10 9 7 5 3 1

Printed in the United States of America

This book was typeset in Bembo.

Candlewick Press
2067 Massachusetts Avenue
Cambridge, Massachusetts 02140

visit us at www.candlewick.com

This book is dedicated to "the other SAS,"
especially Celia Rees and Lee Weatherly,
without whom Emily might still be lost at sea.

Also to my sister, Caroline Kessler,
without whom I would have been pretty lost myself.

And if our hands should meet
in another dream, we shall build
another tower in the sky.

From The Prophet
by Khalil Gibran

Prologue

*I*t's midnight, and as light as day.

A full moon shines down on the ocean, making the waves dance as they skirt the edges of the tiny island, lapping on jagged rocks and stony beaches.

A chariot glides through the sea, tracing a circle around the island. Solid gold and adorned with jewels on every side, the chariot is pulled by dolphins, each decorated with a row of diamonds and pearls along its back and head.

Inside the chariot sits the king of all the oceans: Neptune, grander than ever, a chain of sparkling jewels around his neck, his gold crown glinting above his white hair, his trident by his side. His green eyes shine in the moonlight as he looks across at the island. He is waiting for his bride to appear from the castle that stands above the rocks, half hidden by mist, its dark windows gleaming in the bright night sky.

"Go around again!" he demands, his voice booming like thunder. His words send ripples bouncing away from the chariot. The dolphins draw another circle around the island.

And then she is there, smiling as she steps toward the water's edge, her eyes meeting his, their gaze so fierce it almost brings the space between them to life. A bridge between their two worlds.

A small flock of starlings approaches the water as she does, circling the air above her head like a feathered crown. Twisting her head to smile up at them, she holds out a hand. Instantly, one of the birds breaks off from the circle and flies down toward her open palm. Hovering almost motionless in the air, it drops something from its claw into her palm. A diamond ring. As the woman closes her hand around the ring, the starling rejoins the other birds and they fly away into the night, slinking across the sky like a giant writhing snake.

"I give you this diamond to represent my love, as great as the earth itself, as firm as the ground on which I stand." The woman flicks back shiny black hair as she reaches out toward the chariot to place the ring on Neptune's finger.

A twist of the trident, and a dolphin swims forward. As it bows down to Neptune, it reveals a pearl ring, perfectly balanced on its brow. Neptune takes the ring. Holding it out in his palm, he speaks softly. "And with this pearl, I offer you the sea, my world, as boundless and everlasting as my love for you." He slides the ring onto her finger. "This is a most enchanted moment. A full moon at midnight on the spring equinox. This will not happen for another five hundred years. It is almost as rare as our love."

She smiles at him, her white dress wet at the bottom where she stands in the sea by his chariot.

Holding his trident in the air, Neptune continues. "These rings may only ever be worn by two folk in love—one from the sea, one from land—or by a child of such a pair. As long as they are so worn, no one can remove them."

"No one can even touch them," the woman says.

Neptune laughs. "No one can even touch them," he says. Then he holds his other hand up, palm facing the woman. She does the same and their arms form an arch, the rings touching as they clasp hands. A hundred stars crackle in the sky above them, bursting into color like fireworks. "When the rings touch like this," Neptune continues, "they will undo any act born of hatred or anger. Only love shall reign," he says.

"Only love," she repeats.

Then he spreads his arms out in front of him. "At this moment, night and day are equal, and now, so too are earth and sea. For as long as we wear these rings, the symbols of our marriage, there will always be peace and harmony between the two worlds."

With a final wave of his trident, Neptune reaches out to help the woman into the chariot. Hand in hand, they sit close together, her long dress flowing to one side of the chariot, his jewel-encrusted tail lying over the other side.

The dolphins lift the reins and the chariot glides silently off, taking its royal owners away to begin their married life together.

Chapter One

*E*mily! I won't tell you again."

I opened an eye to see Mom pulling back the curtain across the porthole in my bedroom. Outside, an oval moon hung low in a navy sky. Almost full, I thought automatically. We'd been learning about the moon's cycle at school.

"It's still night," I complained as I pulled the quilt over my face and snuggled back into my pillow.

"It's half past seven," Mom replied, perching on the edge of my bed. She folded the quilt back and kissed my forehead. "Come on, sweet pea," she said. "You'll be late for school." As she got up, she added under her breath, "Not that you'd miss much if you were. They haven't exactly taught you anything useful at that place so far."

She'd left the room before I had a chance to reply.

I let out a heavy sigh as I lay in bed, looking up at the ceiling. Mom seemed to be really down lately. That was the third time she'd grumbled about something in the last week. Personally, I couldn't see what there was to complain about. We were living on a beautiful secret island: Mom, Dad, and me, all together on an elegant old wooden ship half sunk in the golden sand and sparkling water that surround the whole island. Merfolk and humans, together in peace.

I realize that last part isn't necessarily a requirement in everyone's ideal living situation, but it comes in handy when your mom's a human, your dad's a merman, and you're half-and-half.

I pulled my bathing suit on and joined Mom at the breakfast table. As with everything else in our home, the table lay on a slant, so I held on to my cereal bowl as I ate.

Dad swam up to the trapdoor next to my seat and pulled himself up to kiss me on the cheek. "Morning, my little starfish," he said with a smile. "Ready for your ocean studies test?"

"Test me!" I said.

Dad scratched his head. "How big can a giant Japanese spider crab grow?"

"Ten feet," I said instantly.

"Very good. Hm. What color is a banded butterfly fish?"

"Black and silver. Too easy!"

"Too pointless, more like," Mom said under her breath. What was *wrong* with her?

Dad turned to her with a frown. "Not again!" He sighed. "What is the matter with you? Don't you want our daughter to do well at school?"

"I'm sorry," she said, reaching down for Dad's hand. "It's just . . ."

"What? What is it? She's learning a lot; she's enjoying herself, getting good grades. I couldn't be more proud." Dad smiled at me as he talked. I smiled back.

Dad and I hadn't gotten along all that well when we first came to Allpoints Island. I mean, we didn't get along badly; it just wasn't easy. I'd spent most of my life without him, and we didn't really know what to talk about, or where to start.

I didn't know he existed at all till recently. It was only a few months ago that I'd even found out

7

about myself—that I became a mermaid when I went into water. It terrified me in the beginning. The first time it happened, I didn't know what was going on. It was in a school swimming lesson, of all places. But then I got used to it, and I'd sneak out to swim in the sea at night. That's how I met my best friend, Shona. She's a mermaid too. A real, full-time one. She helped me find my dad. When I sneaked into Neptune's prison and saw him for the first time that was the best day of my life.

I guess it all took a little getting used to. But the last few weeks had been fantastic, once all the trouble with the kraken was sorted out. That's the most horrific, fearsome sea monster in the world, and I accidentally woke it up!

Since then, Dad and I had been out swimming together every day, exploring the golden seabed around Allpoints Island, racing against the multicolored fish that fill every stretch of sea around here, playing tag among the coral. Dad was officially the BEST dad in the world.

"That's just it," Mom was saying. "*You* couldn't be more proud. And you have every right to feel proud. Yes, Emily's coming along in leaps and bounds in . . ." She paused to reach over to the pile of textbooks I'd brought home the previous day. I *loved* all my schoolbooks. They weren't like any schoolbooks I'd ever had before, that's for sure! For one thing, they were all made from the coolest shiny materials, or woven with seaweed and decorated with shells and pearls. And, for another, they were in the swishiest subjects! School had never been so much fun.

". . . *Seas and Sirens*," Mom read from the top one. She picked out a couple more books from the pile. "Or *Sailing and Stargazing*, or *Hair Braiding for Modern Mermaids*. I mean!"

"You mean what?" Dad asked, his voice coming out pinched and tight. "Why shouldn't she learn about these things? It's her heritage. What exactly don't you like about it, Mary?"

That's when I knew something was really wrong. No one *ever* calls my mom Mary, least of all Dad. Most people call her Mary P. Her middle name's Penelope, and Dad's always called her Penny—or his lucky Penny, when they're being particularly gooey. Which they hadn't been for a while, now that I thought about it. And while I was thinking about it, I guess Mom had a point. I mean, don't get me wrong. I loved all my new school subjects. But maybe I did sometimes miss some of my old subjects, just a tiny bit. Or just English, perhaps. I used to love writing stories. I even liked spelling tests! That's just because I was good at them.

"What's wrong," said Mom, "is that while *you* may be happy for *your* daughter to learn nothing more than how to brush her hair nicely and tell the

9

time by looking at the clouds, *I'd* like *my* daughter to get a real education."

" 'My daughter,' 'your daughter'? You make it sound as if she's two different people," Dad said. Below the floor I could see the water swishing around as he swirled his tail angrily. It splashed up onto the kitchen floor. Something swished and swirled inside me too, stirred up by his words. Was it true? Was I really two different people?

"Yes, well, maybe she is," Mom snapped, picking up a dish towel and bending down to wipe the floor. They were right. I wasn't like either of them. I was made up of two halves that didn't match. The swirling inside me doubled.

Then Mom glanced up at me and her face softened. "I mean, of course she's not. She's not two different people at all. It's not Emily's fault." Mom smiled at me, reaching up to hold my hands. I snatched them away, turning my face at the same time so I couldn't see the hurt look in her eyes. That's one thing I absolutely can't stand. Her words didn't do much to soothe me, either.

And, anyway, it wasn't fair. She wasn't being fair. I'd never enjoyed school this much in my life! OK—so maybe it would be nice to write stories sometimes, but so what if I wasn't learning social studies and science or fractions and French? Who said there was any point to those either? Was I ever really going to need to know how much John earns in a week if he gets 4 percent commission and 3 percent interest? Surely learning about my surroundings was more important. Knowing which fish were the most dangerous and which were almost friendly. Learning how to look and act like other mermaids, like a *real* mermaid. Even if I did feel a little silly perching on a rock combing my hair sometimes, at least I was learning how to fit in. Didn't Mom care about those things? Didn't she want me to be happy?

I went on eating my breakfast.

Mom drew a breath. "It's just that it's two different worlds," she said in a quiet voice. "And I sometimes wonder if they're just *too* different. I mean, look at my life here. What do I do all day? Sunbathe, comb my hair, maybe go to synchro swim a couple of times a week. This isn't a life for me, Jake. I want more than this."

She'd been saying things like this quite a bit lately. Only last week she'd complained that there was too much ocean and not enough land, and that it made her feel a bit stranded and lonely. I hadn't paid much attention at the time. Perhaps I really should have.

No one spoke for ages. Mom and Dad stared at each other. I'd just taken a spoonful of cereal and didn't want to chew in case it crunched really

loudly, so I sat there with my mouth full of corn-
flakes and milk, waiting for one of them to say
something.

"We'll talk about this later. I need to go out,"
Dad said eventually, and I swallowed my mouthful.
It was too soggy to chew by then, anyway.

Dad left so quickly he didn't even give me a kiss.
Not that I was bothered. I mean, I am twelve. I'll be
thirteen in a couple of months. It's not as if I need
my dad to kiss me good-bye when he goes out!

But. Well, it showed something. Maybe this was
all my fault. It was only because of me that they
had to try to bring the two worlds together at all.
That and the fact that they loved each other, of
course. But maybe they didn't anymore. Maybe
they'd grown away from each other so much in the
twelve years they'd been apart that they didn't love
each other at all now and had to stay together just
because of me. And maybe they both hated it, and
hated each other, and in the end they'd both end
up hating me too. And now Mom didn't even like
her life anymore!

A strange, cold feeling started to spread inside me,
creeping around my body, seeping into my bones.
Only weeks ago, we'd been given a new start on this

island. A dream come true. Everything we'd ever wanted. But what if it wasn't a dream come true at all? What if it was going to turn into a nightmare, as so many of my dreams did? Or used to.

A small voice inside my head said I was probably blowing it out of proportion. *It's just an argument,* I reasoned with myself. *All married couples argue.* And I knew I had a vivid imagination. My teachers had always told me so. Part of me knew I was over-reacting. But the other part of me couldn't stop worrying. And that part seemed to have a louder voice.

Perhaps it was only a matter of time before Mom and Dad decided to abandon ship and not bother being together at all. Then what? Would I have to choose between them? Would either of them even want me if it was all because of me that their marriage had gone wrong? They'd probably fight each other *not* to have me.

I tried to shake the thoughts from my mind as I got ready for school. The ocean studies test was that afternoon and I was determined to do well. I'd show Dad that I really could follow in his footsteps, or wash in his wake, as he liked to say.

The thought cheered me up, and I even allowed myself to smile as I packed my books. Till another thought chased the smile off my face like a shark chasing off a shoal of unsuspecting bar jacks.

The better I did in my mermaid lessons, the less

time I was spending on land with Mom doing what she liked. The closer I got to Dad, the further away I moved from her. Now that I thought about it, I wasn't surprised she was unhappy. I'd been so busy getting to know Dad, I'd hardly done anything with Mom. I should have listened when she'd told me she was lonely. I should have made Dad listen too. Why hadn't I?

I didn't have an answer. So perhaps she was right after all. Perhaps the two worlds were simply too different to coexist. Perhaps my parents weren't meant to be together at all.

I slunk away from the boat, dropping into the water without even saying good-bye, too miserable to speak, too scared to think.

Chapter Two

*A*s I dived down, my worries melted away, falling off me as if I were shedding a skin. My legs felt as heavy as concrete, for a moment weighing me down in the water as they stiffened. It didn't bother me, though. I was used to it. In fact, it was the best feeling in the world because I knew what was going to happen next.

My legs joined together, sticking to each other so tightly it was as though someone were taping them together and winding bandages around and around them.

And then my tail formed.

I stretched out like a cat and watched as the bottom half of my bathing suit faded into shiny silver scales, glinting and sparkling and spreading farther and farther as my tail flickered and swished to life. I would never get bored of that feeling. It was like having been shut up in a box and then taking the lid off and throwing the sides open and being told you could move wherever you wanted, however you wanted. It was like having the whole world opened up to you.

I hovered in the water, flicking my tail to make sure it had fully formed. It glinted purple and green as I batted away a pair of tiny silver fish swimming along its side. Every toss sent little bubbles dancing up to the surface.

I let myself sigh happily. Everything felt better while I was a mermaid.

I swam along the tops of the coral, glancing down at the underwater forests as I made my way to school.

Bright green bushes waved at me as I sailed over them; rubbery red tubes nodded and bobbed from side to side. A pair of golden sea horses weaved their way around long trails of reeds that swayed and dipped in the current, their tails entwined. Gangs of paper-thin fish with bright yellow tails and round-bellied blue fish with black eyes all darted purposefully around me. I tried to remember what they were all called, just in case it came up on the ocean studies test, but they weren't familiar. There was something new to see here every day. I could never tire of Allpoints Island, even if Mom had had enough of the place.

I came to a cluster of rocks at the edge of a tunnel and waited. School was at the other end of the tunnel, in the Emerald Caves. Shona and I had started meeting up here so we could go in together.

A few of the others from my class smiled as they went past me. Most of the class were mermaids. There were a few merboys and two human boys and two girls. I hadn't gotten to know that many of the others yet, although Shona and I hung around quite a lot with two other mermaids, Althea and Marina. I was the only one who was half-and-half. The only semi-mer. There was a name for us, even if there were hardly any of us in existence!

I'd gotten used to being the only one, I suppose, even though I sometimes wished I weren't. It would just be so cool to have someone else who knew what it felt like to transform like I did. It would be better than cool, in fact. It might help me feel that I fit into the world somewhere, that I wasn't quite such a total misfit.

Well, there was *one* person. The only other one like me I'd ever met, but he hardly counted. For one thing, he was an adult; for another, he was the most untrustworthy, sly person you could ever meet: Mr. Beeston. My mom's so-called friend. Who'd turned out to be so much of a friend that he'd spent years spying on us and reporting back to Neptune!

Anyway, that was all history now. At least he wasn't trying to drug us or lie to us anymore.

"Emily!" A familiar voice tinkled across to me, sending Mr. Beeston far from my mind. Shona!

She swam toward me, clutching her tote bag against her side. It was silver and gold and covered in tiny pink shells. Shona always had the prettiest things. She was the kind of mermaid you imagine mermaids to be, all girly and sparkly, with shiny long blond hair. Not like me. I was trying to grow my hair, and it was past my shoulders now, but it still never looked anything like Shona's: sleek and beautiful and, well, mermaidlike, I guess.

"Have you studied?" she asked excitedly as we followed behind a group of younger mermaids with their moms. Holding hands with one another as they swam, they raced ahead to their class, leaving their moms chatting as they glided along behind them.

"Dad tested me this morning," I replied. "Think I got them all, but I don't know if I've learned the right fish."

"We have till this afternoon, anyway," Shona said. "And you know what this morning is, don't you?"

I smiled as I answered her. "Beauty and Deport-ment. What else?"

B&D was Shona's favorite class. Nothing made her happier than learning a new way to style her hair or get the best shine out of her tail or swim with perfect elegance. I was more interested in shipwreck studies and siren stories, but the whole idea of mermaid school was still so new to me that I didn't really mind what we did or what we learned, as long as it wasn't long division!

We swam on down the channel. You had to feel your way along the walls as you swam along the first part. My heart rate always sped up here. The walls, slimy and wet and cold, set off too many memories of what had happened when I'd discovered the kraken in a slimy, dark tunnel.

We soon rounded a corner, and the tunnel opened up again, growing lighter and filling with color. I smiled away the memories. I never told Shona how I felt going along that channel. I always wondered if she felt the same way, but it was something we never talked about. She'd been with me when I woke the kraken and was probably as eager as I was to forget about it.

We bumped into Althea and Marina as we reached the fork that led down to our class. Marina swam hurriedly over to us, her long gold tail flicking rapidly from side to side. "Hey, I overheard Miss Finwave talking to one of the moms on the way in," she said with a grin. "And guess what?"

Shona's eyes opened wide, glistening even more than they usually did. "What?" she replied in the same excited tone as Marina's.

"We're going on a B and D outing!"

"Swishy!"

Althea turned to me. I must have looked puzzled. "It means we get to go out exploring the reef and the rocks," she explained.

"What, you mean like when we studied the creeks through the island?"

She shook her head. "That was a geography reef trip. More scientific. This one will probably have something to do with looking for material to make new hairbrushes or finding the perfect rocks to sit on the edge of." Althea pretended to yawn as she spoke.

Marina punched her arm and laughed. "Come on, you know you love it," she said.

Althea grinned back at her friend. "Yeah, I suppose it beats this afternoon's OS test."

We went on talking as we followed the fork that led up to our classroom. It still took my breath away every time I arrived here. A cave filled with smooth greeny-blue water. Above, shimmering stalactites drooped from the high ceiling in thin folds like pterodactyls' wings or pointed down to the pool like sharp bundles of arrows frozen in midflight. All around us, blue and green and purple lights glimmered and winked, dancing on the surface of the deep pool. We swam into the cave, taking our places among the rest of the class.

At the front of the pool, a long scroll hung from the ceiling. It always had a message for us in swirly, loopy writing when we arrived. Today it read:

Emerald Class:
Please remember that we have a test this afternoon. This morning, you will not need reeds and scrolls, so don't unpack your bags. Leave them somewhere safe for now and please wait for me to arrive.

Underneath it was signed *Miss R. Finwave*.

"Told you!" said Marina. "We must be going out first thing."

A moment later, Miss Finwave arrived and the class hushed instantly. Her blond hair shone as she swam into the class. It trailed all the way down her back, glistening and perfectly combed. Her tail was sleek, thin, and pale pink, with tiny gold stars all along it. It hardly twitched when she moved. She always seemed to glide rather than swim.

She was one of the prettiest of the adult mermaids

on the island, and one of the youngest. We always took note of her and tried to do what she said—and tried to stay in her good graces. She knew exactly when to praise and when to tell someone off. And she did the praise so nicely and the telling-off so sharply that we all knew which one we wanted to get more of.

I patted down my hair and tried to sit up straight. We were all perched on rocks just under the surface. Shona always looked exactly like the mermaids in textbooks. I tried to copy her but usually slipped off the edge or got pins and needles in my tail from sitting awkwardly.

"Excellent, Shona," Miss Finwave said as she looked around the classroom. "Lovely posture, as always." She glanced at me. "Nice try, Emily. Coming along quite well there."

I couldn't keep the edges of my mouth from twitching into a smile. I know that "nice try" isn't exactly a gold medal, but it's better than a telling-off for slouching, which was what one of the boys behind me got.

"Let's have straight backs, please, Adam," she said as she glanced around. A moment later, she nodded. "Much better."

Once she was happy that we all looked our best and were paying attention, Miss Finwave folded her arms and surveyed the class. "Now then, children," she said. "This is a very important day. Can anyone guess what is important about today?"

One of the mermaids in my row put her hand up. "Is it the ocean studies test?" she asked.

Miss Finwave smiled gently. "Good girl, Morag. I'm glad you remembered the test," she said. "But that's not what I'm thinking of. Anyone else?"

Shona raised her hand. "Is it the Beauty and Deportment outing?" she asked shyly.

Miss Finwave pursed her lips. "Well, who told you we were doing anything like that?"

Shona blushed, but before she had a chance to say anything, Miss Finwave continued. "In a roundabout way, it has something to do with that. I shall explain. In fact, I have a very important announcement to make."

Then she lowered her voice so that she sounded even more authoritative than usual. "We are extremely privileged at Allpoints Island to be receiving a visit from our king today."

She paused as the class erupted in gasps and whispers. "All right, that's enough, thank you," she said firmly. The classroom hushed instantly.

"Now then, I am not at liberty to tell you too many details about this visit. Normally a visit from our king would be preceded by many weeks of preparation. This visit is different. It has been kept secret under Neptune's strict orders. What I can tell you, though, is that a few of the adults in positions of responsibility here at Allpoints have been asked to conduct some extremely important work." She smiled proudly. "I am one of those adults," she said, "and I have decided to enlist your help. That is why he is visiting us. I just heard the news this morning. Aren't we lucky, children?"

She beamed around at us all. Most of the class stared back at her with wide eyes, excitement shining on their faces. All I could think was, *Not Neptune. Not here. Please, no.* I'd met Neptune only twice, and both times it had led to trouble. BIG trouble.

"I thought it would be nice to combine this project with a Beauty and Deportment lesson," Miss Finwave continued. "You will, I'm sure, be as delighted and honored as I am to hear the news of this visit."

I gulped.

"And I am confident that you will make me proud," Miss Finwave went on. "I know you will be as polite and well behaved as you can for our most distinguished guest."

She looked around the class as though assessing her opinion of us, just to make sure that she was right and could trust us to behave, or daring us to prove her wrong.

Her eyes fell on me. "I know you won't let me down," she said sternly. I didn't know if she was talking to the whole class or just me. There was no way I would let anyone down, though. I'd nearly gotten myself imprisoned the first time I met Neptune and was nearly crushed to death by a sea monster the second time. I'd melt into the background and keep my mouth shut this time, for sure. He wouldn't even know I was there.

Miss Finwave nodded. "Listen carefully, all of you, so you understand what to do. For now, all you need to know is that we are looking for jewels."

"Might have known," Althea whispered to me. "Why else would Neptune come here, if it wasn't for gold or treasure? What else does he care about?"

"Thank you, girls," Miss Finwave said with a sharp glance in our direction.

"Sorry, Miss Finwave," we replied mechanically as half the class turned to stare at us.

"We will split up into small groups, and each group will choose a small area of the island and its surroundings, particularly the bays and beaches," she said. "You are searching primarily for crystals, gold, that kind of thing. But you will also search for anything you can find with which to adorn yourself in some way. That is where B and D comes in. Remember, children, you are dressing to meet your king!"

I glanced at Shona. She was smiling as though

someone had just told her she'd won the lottery. If mermaids have a lottery, which I don't think they do.

"You will use all you have been studying this term in B and D and combine this with a bit of initiative and a touch of local knowledge. Then you will come back to class and share your findings. There will be a gold starfish for whoever finds the finest jewel, and another for the best-decorated child, when we return. Remember, use anything you can to enhance your appearance just that little bit—for our guest, for me, for each other, and, most important, for yourselves. Now, any questions?"

Shona and I decided to go out on our own. We picked North Bay. That's where I lived with Mom and Dad on *Fortuna*. There is something about our bay that seems to sparkle more than all the others. I was pretty sure anything glittery would wash up there eventually. Also, it has more boats than the other bays. Shona reckoned that made it a good place to find things, as there were so many nooks and crannies around the underside of the boats where lost jewels could easily get stuck. Some of the oldest boats were lived in; most were abandoned and unused.

Millie lived in North Bay too, on our old boat, *The King of the Sea*. Millie is Mom's best friend who came with us to Allpoints Island. She used to have a kiosk called Palms on the Pier in Brightport, where we lived before we came here. Recently she'd started doing tarot readings and hypnotism for some of the mer-families because they were so impressed with the way she helped deal with the kraken by hypnotizing it. She's a funny one, Millie. Most of the time, she's obviously the world's biggest phony, but just occasionally she gets something right and you have to take back everything you've said about her.

I thought it might be a good idea to search near her, as she always had crystal balls and fancy jewelry herself. Perhaps she'd dropped something over the side that we could use.

Shona swam ahead. She was determined to win the gold starfish for best-decorated mermaid. I went along with her, too distracted to concentrate properly. Neptune. In our classroom. Today!

"Imagine, Neptune coming to our class!" Shona said, reading my thoughts, as she so often did.

"Yeah, imagine that," I said, without any of her enthusiasm. I thought back to the times I'd met him so far and how I'd managed to get on his wrong side both times. Not that he was especially known for having much of a right side.

We had an hour before we had to get back to class with our findings. Gliding silently into the bay, I scoured the seabed for anything that could be used as a mermaid accessory. It wasn't the kind of thing I normally bothered with, but I wanted to try to look the part, at least, for Miss Finwave, and for Neptune. And Shona was so excited by the whole idea, I didn't want to dampen her enthusiasm.

Mostly the seabed was just pure white sand, soft and powdery. Every now and then we swam over a rock. We'd dive down and scrabble around it, coming back up with lengths of golden seaweed to wrap around our tails, or shells that had holes worn right through the middle. Great for necklaces, if we could just find a thin chain somewhere.

"Come on, let's try this one." Shona swam ahead toward an old fishing boat that lay wrecked on the seabed.

We swam over the top of it. The front end had been smashed against a huge rocky layer of coral and lay exposed and ruined. Algae and seaweed had grown around it over the years. Groups of fish swam in and out of the wreckage that had become part of their habitat. Two black-and-white harlequins pecked at the rotting wood, covered as it must be by now with the tiniest forms of sea life, perhaps a small breakfast for this pair. A lone parrot fish swam into the hull of the boat. We followed it in.

"Nothing much here," I said as we looked under the frayed benches and all around the edges of the boat.

"Hey, look at this." Shona swam into the wheelhouse of the boat. Spongy coral had somehow made its way in, filling the little room as though it were a greenhouse. Shona was pulling at some delicate purple sea fans. "I could wear them in my hair," she said, holding one up against her head. It looked like a feathery hat.

"Nice," I said, tugging at a blue-and-pink vase sponge. "Hey, maybe we could use this in class. Miss Finwave could put flowers in it."

"Swishy idea!" Shona grinned.

Pink jellyfish lined the bottom of the boat. "Shame they're poisonous," Shona said as we swam back out into the bay with our findings. "They would have made nice cushions."

I laughed. "Where to next?"

"How about your boat?"

"*Fortuna?*"

Shona nodded happily. "It's so old I bet all sorts of things have gotten lodged underneath it over the years."

"OK. And then *King*," I insisted. "I want to see if we can find any of Millie's discarded lucky pebbles!"

"Come on," Shona said. "Let's go."

29

We swam all around the edges of *Fortuna*. Portholes lined the lower level. Some had glass in them. The biggest one near the front, the one Dad and I used for getting in and out of the boat, didn't. The whole lower floor was half submerged. That was how Mom and Dad managed to live there together.

Green ferns reached up all around the front end of the boat. It was like an underwater garden, except that we never had to water it!

"Let's take some of these," Shona said, grabbing at the ferns. She held them against her tail. "We can wear them as skirts."

Under the ferns I spotted some silver seaweed, thin and wispy. It was just the thing to help turn our shells into necklaces. I carefully ripped out some strands.

Swimming around the boat, we scavenged under the rocks, trailed along the hull with our fingers, batted fat red fish out of our way, and created sandstorms as we burrowed for treasure, picking up anything colorful that we could carry.

"Come on," Shona said. "We've got enough of the B and D stuff. I really want to find some of the jewels. Think how pleased Neptune would be!"

"Hm," I said. It was hard to imagine Neptune being pleased about *anything,* let alone something I'd done.

"Let's try *King*," Shona said. Then she stretched out her long tail and swam off. I started to follow her—but something was drawing me away. It was as if I was being pulled in another direction by something attached to me, tugging at me. What was it?

"Shona, let's try over there," I said without even knowing why. I pointed toward a bunch of rocks nestled among a tiny forest of bushes and reeds. Spiky black anemones sat along the rocks' edges, lining them like guards. The bushes were gray and dull.

"There won't be anything down there."

"Please," I said, my chest aching with the need to look in the rocks. "Let's just try it."

Shona sighed. "Come on, then."

She scavenged away under the rocks with me, dodging the anemones and burrowing into the sand without knowing why we were looking here any more than I did. A small sandstorm built up around us as we scratched and scrabbled at the seabed, digging out broken shells and pebbles. But nothing more than that.

"How about this?" Shona asked, holding up a razor shell. "It would do for a comb, perhaps, if we just cut away a few ridges." She turned the shell over in her hands, held it to her hair.

I nodded. "Yeah," I said absentmindedly. But I

knew there was something else there. I could feel it shining into me, almost calling me. It reminded me of a game we used to play where someone hides an object and the others have to look for it. Move nearer, you get warmer. Move away and you're cold again. *Warmer, warmer.* I could feel it close to me. What was it?

"Come on, let's try one more boat," Shona said. "We need to be back in class soon." She started to swim away.

"Wait," I called.

Shona turned. "What is it?"

Could I really say what I felt? That I had a burning in my chest that told me I had to stay here, had to find whatever it was that was down here? Look what had happened the last time I made Shona help me follow my instincts. We'd ended up disturbing the kraken and threatening the safety of the whole island. No, I couldn't do it.

But I couldn't leave it alone either.

"You go on," I said. "I'll just look around a bit more here."

"But there's nothing to see. It's just a bunch of rocks, Em."

"I know. I just—I just want one more look around."

Shona flicked her hair back. "OK, if you're sure. I'll meet you by *King*. Don't be long."

"Great. See you there," I said, trying to return her smile. I hurried back to my task as soon as she'd turned away. What was down here? Why was it drawing me in? One way or another, I was determined to find out.

I worked like a dog burrowing down a hole on the trail of a rabbit. I scratched my tail on the coral, my hair was matted and tangled, and my nails were filled with sand and broken from tearing at the rocks. But I couldn't stop. I had to find it. Whatever was down here, I needed to find it. I could almost feel it calling me, as though it *wanted* me to find it.

"What are you doing?"

I jerked my head up. Shona!

"I—"

"I've been waiting for ages. I thought you were going to meet me at *King*."

"I was," I said. "I just—I wanted to—"

"Your nails!" Shona screeched. I instantly curled my hands into fists, but it was too late. Shona swam over to me and uncurled them. "Miss Finwave's going to hit the waves!"

"Yeah, I know," I mumbled. I didn't want to talk about my nails! I wanted to get back to my search.

"Come on," Shona said, "we're going to be late." She had some fine, wispy pink seaweed draped around her neck. She must have found it by *King*.

"All right," I said. I didn't make any effort to move. Shona pursed her lips and pulled her hair to the side. "Emily, what's going on? You're acting all weird."

"No, I'm fine," I said with a lame smile. "Really. Sorry. Come on—let's go."

I dragged myself away from the hole, pretending I was going back to class with Shona. There was no way I was leaving this, though.

"Hang on a sec," I said as we passed *Fortuna*. "I'll just go in and clean my nails."

"What?" Shona flicked her tail impatiently.

"Because of Miss Finwave." I faltered. "I won't be long. I'll just go in. I'll be right behind you."

"I'll wait." Shona sighed.

"No. You go ahead. I'll catch up. I don't want you to be late."

She shrugged. "OK," she said, and swam away.

As soon as she was out of sight, I went straight back to the rocks. Whatever was down there was pulling me so hard I could almost feel it, as though I were a fish caught on a piece of bait. As I burrowed deeper and searched all over, I almost had to hold my hand over my heart to stop it from hurting.

And then I saw it.

I turned over one final stone and there it was, glinting at me, throwing light in a multicolored arc all around. I gasped.

A ring. A thick gold band with the biggest, brightest diamond I had ever seen in my life. It must have been in an accident, because the band had been dented and bent out of shape. I squeezed it onto my middle finger and examined it. I could tell that it used to be much bigger, but with all the dents, it fit my finger perfectly. Looking down at it, I had the strangest sensation. It was like a tight knot inside me that made me want to scream or cry or laugh, I didn't know which. All of them.

I could have stared at it all day. But I had to get back. Glancing down at my hand every few seconds just to check that the ring was still there, for some reason I couldn't help smiling to myself as I swam back to class.

Chapter Three

I joined the rest of the class, huddled around a huge, flat rock in the center of the pool, where we examined our multicolored findings. I'd managed to sneak in while Miss Finwave was looking away, so she didn't notice I'd gotten back after everyone else.

The rock was covered with a collection that lit up the classroom, splashing a hundred colors all around us. I stared at it. Seaweed in bright pinks and greens, shells with the prettiest swirling patterns, sea flowers of every color, ancient jars filled with sand so bright it was more like glitter.

Bright blue and green and orange crystals, shining white rocks. Neptune was going to be very pleased.

When Miss Finwave noticed me hanging back at the edge of the pool, she did a double take. Her face turned pale. "Shooting sharks, Emily!" she said, clasping a hand over her mouth.

"What?"

"Your hair!" She gasped, looking around frantically. "Quick, someone get me a comb! Hurry!"

"Here, she can use mine," Marina said, pulling a razor-shell comb out of her rope bag.

"Thank you, Marina," Miss Finwave said tightly as she proceeded to pull at the tangles in my hair, yanking my head again and again till the comb ran smoothly through.

"That's better," she said, examining me. "Now, let's see your contribution."

My hand was in my pocket. I was about to bring it out to show her the ring, but the strangest thing happened. The ring seemed to be weighing my hand down. I could almost hear it, begging me not to show it to Miss Finwave.

"Shona's already put our things out," I said, pointing to the sea fans and shells she'd collected while she was with me. I held my breath while I waited for the reply. My hand still firmly in my pocket, I twisted the ring around on my finger so

I could feel the diamond against my palm. Then I curled my fingers around it. Safe.

Miss Finwave simply nodded. "Very good. Nice work, you two," she said quickly, before moving on to someone else.

I let my breath out with a sigh. Then I glanced over to see Shona staring at me. "What's going on?" she whispered.

"Tell you later," I whispered back. "I found something!" Now that I'd managed to find out what it was without getting Shona in trouble, I couldn't wait to share it with her!

Shona's eyes went all round and big, but before she had the chance to reply, Miss Finwave had snapped her tail to get everyone's attention.

"Now then, children," she said, "well done. You have created quite a treasure trove in here! Neptune *will* be pleased with you. He'll be with us very shortly, and I want each one of you to adorn yourself with your findings, making yourself as beautiful or as handsome as you can. And the politest class I have ever had, please. Is that understood?"

We replied with a synchronized "Yes, Miss Finwave" and then erupted into a scuffle of noise as we shared and compared our findings, bartering and bargaining with one another to get the best combinations of colors, textures, and patterns.

I looked around the pool at what we'd managed to do with our appearances. It was incredible how a few bits and pieces from the ocean floor had transformed every one of us. Althea had created extensions from some bright blue seaweed. Next to her jet-black hair, they made her look gothic and glamorous. Marina had made a starfish brooch for her bikini top and a belt from oyster shells. Adam had attached a shiny silver crab's husk to some black ship's rope to make a belt that could have been worn by a rock star. Shona and I made bangles and necklaces from the shells we'd picked up, wove the fans into hats, stuck shiny stones in patterns on our tails and surrounded them with swirling patterns made from glittery pink sand. We laid all the jewels we'd found on the rock in the center of the classroom.

"Not bad, not bad at all," Miss Finwave said with a satisfied smile as she examined us. "Very good work. You should all feel as proud as piranhas."

Just then, a strange thing happened. Strange— but familiar. Horribly familiar. The classroom started to shake. The water in the pool bubbled and frothed. Stalactites shivered and wobbled above us, threatening to crash down and spear any one of us.

The last time it had happened, I'd thought it was an earthquake. But it wasn't. At least I knew what it was this time.

"Here comes Neptune," Miss Finwave called above the noise of water swirling around and around, creating a whirlpool. "Get to the sides, children. It'll stop in a moment."

Don't panic. Relax. I tried to breathe smoothly. But my breath came out in sharp, spiky puffs.

He isn't coming to see me. I haven't done anything wrong, I told myself again and again. I'd make sure I didn't have a scale out of place this time. He wouldn't even know I was there.

We swam to the side of the pool, falling over ourselves and one another and barely managing to keep our new accessories in place.

And then the water calmed just as suddenly as it had started. The pool shone brighter than ever; the walls glistened and gleamed; the cave was silent as we waited.

The dolphins came first, swimming into the pool in a row as straight as an army's front line. Behind them, Neptune's chariot slid smoothly into view. Gold, grand, and adorned with a thousand jewels, it snatched my breath away every time I saw it. I had to shield my eyes from the dazzling light it shone around the cave.

The class fell even more silent. And then there he was. Neptune. In our classroom! Sitting back in his chariot, his golden crown on his head, his trident held high, his beard reaching down to his chest, and the deepest frown on his face, Neptune arrived in the cave.

As the chariot came to a halt, the dolphins immediately swam around to the back and lined up along the opposite side of the pool from us.

Without speaking, Neptune raised both hands in the air. Holding the trident aloft in one hand, he snapped his fingers twice with the other. A second later, someone else swam into the pool. We couldn't see who it was at first. He had his head down, reverently bowing to Neptune. But as soon as he raised it, I gasped. I'd know that face anywhere: the broken teeth, the odd eyes, the creepy sideways looks.

Mr. Beeston.

Neptune nodded to him and he swam to the edge of the chariot. "Your Majesty," he said in a deep voice, "please allow me to attend to your wishes. Whatever it is you need, you know you only have to—"

Neptune banged his trident impatiently on the floor of the chariot. "Enough!" he bellowed.

Miss Finwave swam forward and bowed her head. "Your Majesty, it is an honor," she said simply. "I have taken your orders very seriously and have set about my work, enlisting the help of the children, as I told you—"

Neptune raised an eyebrow into a wide, white arch above his eye.

Miss Finwave went on quickly. "We have merely begun some collections in your honor. They have not been told the *reason* for these collections."

Neptune sniffed. "Very well," he said. Then he snapped his fingers and motioned for Mr. Beeston to come toward him. Mr. Beeston swam forward again, simpering and drooling like the creep that he is.

"Explain to the children why I am here," Neptune said to him.

"I — certainly, your Majesty," Mr. Beeston stammered. "Right away." Then he pulled on his crooked tie and cleared his throat before swimming toward us. Flicking his tail to propel himself higher in the water, he glanced back at the chariot. A brief glower from Neptune was all the encouragement he needed to get started.

"Children," he began, smiling around at us with his horrible creepy smile, "as you know, Allpoints Island is a very special and important place. For many reasons. And one of those reasons is the kraken."

A sound like thunder boomed into the cave. I looked around to see what it was. No one else seemed to have noticed it. They were all looking at Mr. Beeston.

There it was again.

That was when I realized it was my heart, beating so loud I could feel it thud in my ears. The kraken. Neptune's sea monster. Had something happened to it? Had it awoken again? That was the absolute worst thing he could possibly have come to tell us. Not only would it mean we were all in danger again, but Neptune would remember whose fault it was, who had released it in the first place. I slunk low in the water, trying to hide, trying to make myself invisible. I could feel my face heating up. As it did, the ring seemed to burn in my pocket, spreading heat through my fingers, which were still folded tightly around the diamond.

"As you all know, the kraken was disturbed recently." Mr. Beeston paused and looked me directly in the eye. Why couldn't I make myself invisible? *Why?*

Then he looked away again, surveying the whole class. "Well then. Since that time, I am pleased to say that, as the chief kraken keeper, I have ensured that no further disturbances have taken place. I have regarded my duties with the utmost vigilance, loyalty, and—"

"Beeston!" Neptune growled.

"I'm sorry, Your Majesty," Mr. Beeston said, twisting to bow low again. Turning back to the class, he continued. "However, there are one or two unresolved matters from that sorry period. Not everything is exactly as it should be."

43

"GET TO THE POINT!" Neptune exploded, shaking the cave so much that a rock fell from its perch and splashed into the water, spraying us all.

Reddening, Mr. Beeston spoke quickly. "The kraken held many jewels in its lair. The spoils of many a warship, the cargo of many a cruiser, were safely buried and out of danger while it slept. But since the recent troubles, some of these treasures have become dislodged. Items that were buried deep, deep, down in the caves under Allpoints Island have emerged or been dispersed."

Mr. Beeston stopped and closed his eyes. Then, continuing more quietly, he said, "Most have been recovered. I have made sure of that. Entrusted with such an important task, I would not have dared fail. However, I—"

"Beeston, that is ENOUGH!" Neptune rose in his chariot. With his head towering high above us all, it seemed he was almost as tall as the ceiling. "I shall continue. Then maybe the children will understand what has happened here. And WHY."

Pointing at Mr. Beeston with his trident, he said, "Certain folk have let me down. Those entrusted with the highest of honors have allowed the privilege of my trust to slip through their fins. And as a result, I have lost some of the treasure that is rightly mine. This is not a situation I am prepared to endure."

He paused, looking around the silent classroom.

"I want it back," he said eventually in a voice as quiet and as threatening as a rumble of thunder from miles away. "Every last jewel, every last coin. All of it."

I felt my hand burning up as though it were on fire. The ring! It was scorching a hole through my palm. It was as though it was trying to tell me something. But what? It was so strange. One moment it made me feel happy and at peace; the next, it sent my heart racing like an engine. I tried to lift it out of my pocket, but I couldn't! My hand was jammed fast and wouldn't budge. I bit hard into my cheek to take my mind off the sensation.

Just then, Miss Finwave swam forward. "Your Majesty," she said, "please allow me to show you what we have collected for you." She motioned to us to clear a path toward the rock in the center of the pool and waved a hand out toward it. Treasure winked and sparkled from every inch of the rock.

"The children have done well, wouldn't you agree?" Miss Finwave said, turning to Neptune.

But he wasn't listening. His eyes feasted greedily on the jewels as he swam all the way around the rock. "Perfect," he said, his mouth dribbling slightly, his eyes glinting as much as the jewels. Reaching out with both arms, he swept the multicolored gems toward him, clutching them to his chest.

As he glided back to his chariot, his hands crammed with jewels, he turned back to us. "Well done, children," he said. "You've done the island proud. Miss Finwave, excellent thinking. I wonder if anyone else who was set this task has fared so well. I shall visit them all and reward the most conscientious. Now that I am here to oversee this operation and ensure no one attempts to trick me out of my treasure, I will no longer keep it confidential. You may speak freely of your task. And you may be proud of your work."

His eyes leaving the jewels for only seconds at a time, Neptune looked around at us all. I'm sure he stared directly at me when he spoke again. "It will all be returned. Every last item. Do you hear me?"

With one final, terrible stare at all of us, Neptune banged his trident loudly on the floor of his chariot. The row of dolphins returned in a flash, picking up the reins in their mouths. Now that he had a chariot full of jewels, he wasn't interested in us.

"Beeston, wrap it up," he called over his shoulder. "Return to me if you have any more news on my lost treasure. And not before."

With that, the dolphins swam into action, whisking Neptune out of the cave.

Once Neptune had left, Mr. Beeston seemed to swim higher in the water. When he spoke to us again, his voice contained the old creepy snarl I knew so well rather than the simpering tone that he adopted whenever Neptune was around.

"You have heard your king," he said, looking slowly around at us all. "I do not need to tell you how powerful he is. When he says he wants something to happen, it will happen. It will indeed. And I, my friends"—he raised a hand to smooth down his hair—"I shall make sure of that. Now that this mission is no longer secret, every single inhabitant of this island will take part in this project until our king is satisfied. Do you hear me?"

We all nodded. Most of the others looked too nervous to speak. I wasn't nervous, just annoyed. Who did he think he was, telling us what to do like that? He didn't frighten *me*!

Just then, Mr. Beeston's gaze fell on me. He looked into my eyes, then glanced toward the pocket at the side of my tail. Did he know? Should I tell him now? I tried to pull my hand out. Again it felt chained down. I couldn't even move it! What if I could never move my hand again? The panic must have shown in my eyes as Mr. Beeston swam closer to me. "Got something to share, Emily?" he asked, his voice as slimy and ugly as a conger eel.

"No!" I said quickly. What else could I say? *Well, yes, possibly, but it appears to be a magic ring that is digging into my palm, holding my hand down so I can't actually show it to you just at this moment?* I don't think so.

47

He swam closer. "Are you sure? I hope you know how seriously Neptune would view it if anyone tried to trick him out of anything, even the smallest jewel. . . ."

That was when I lost my nerve. Why? Why did I let him get to me? Why couldn't I just brush away his words and his sneering manner and threatening tone? Or perhaps it had more to do with the reminder of what it was like to be on the receiving end of Neptune's anger.

"I—I found something," I said.

He moved closer. "Found something?"

"A—a ring." I could sense Shona next to me, almost feel her eyes staring at me—almost hear the question in her mind. I didn't look at her.

"What kind of ring?" he asked.

I would have shown it to him. I *would* have. I'd have handed it over on the spot if I could. But I couldn't. The ring felt like a claw, gripping my palm, pinning my hand to my pocket. "A diamond," I said, feeling warmth flood through me as I thought about the ring. "A huge diamond. All shiny and sparkly—the most beautiful diamond ring you've ever seen."

Mr. Beeston sniffed. "There was no such ring in the collection," he said, starting to swim away from me.

"And it had a thick gold band that was battered and twisted out of shape," I called to his retreating

48

back. Now that I'd started talking about the ring, I couldn't stop myself from saying more. A second later I wished I had, as Mr. Beeston stopped and turned. "Wait a minute!" His face had gone gray. "Diamond, you say?" he sputtered.

I nodded.

"A huge diamond, a battered gold band?"

I nodded again.

"Battered as though it had been thrown away, discarded?"

"As though it had been through a war!" I said.

Mr. Beeston swallowed and wiped a strand of hair from his face. "I don't believe it," he said. "That must be the—" Then he stopped. "Where is it?" he hissed quietly, close to my ear.

One last time, I tried to lift my hand. I couldn't do it. What was I going to do? I couldn't say that the ring wouldn't let me take my hand out of my pocket! How utterly ridiculous would that sound? No one would believe me, let alone Mr. Beeston. And, anyway, I could sense it, feel it, trying to pull me back, shut me up.

"I lost it," I said eventually.

"Lost it?" Mr. Beeston spluttered. "*Lost* it? You can't have lost it!"

"I dropped it in the sand. Sorry," I said, turning my face away and praying he wouldn't notice my reddening cheeks. They felt almost as hot as the ring, still burning a hole in my hand.

He swam closer. "Let me see your—"

At that moment, Miss Finwave swam in between us. "Mr. Beeston, in case you hadn't noticed, the children gathered plenty of jewels for Neptune. And he seemed perfectly happy with our work. So I would be very grateful if you could please acknowledge our efforts just a little bit and leave us to get on with our school day. We have a lot to do."

"Very well," Mr. Beeston said. With a curt bow to the teacher, he swam to the edge of the pool, toward the tunnel that led out of the cave. Turning back toward us when he reached the tunnel's entrance, he added, "Thank you, children," and smiled.

Then Miss Finwave flicked the end of her tail in a loud snap to get our attention, and everyone turned back to face her. Everyone except me. I was still looking at Mr. Beeston. He was still looking at me. "We're not done yet," he mouthed. "You'll see."

And with that, he swam off and disappeared into the darkness of the tunnel.

I pretended to listen like the rest of the class as Miss Finwave started to talk about the afternoon's test. I pretended I didn't care about Mr. Beeston's silly threats or Neptune's anger or any of it. Neptune had been here to see us all, not just me. And Mr. Beeston hadn't really whispered a threat to me as he left. Not really. I must have misread his lips, or he was talking to someone else. It was just me imagining things again.

I gripped the ring for comfort. At least I had that.

And if it felt as though it glowed and burned on my finger, reaching out for me with a sharpness that almost cut through me—well, surely I was imagining that too.

Chapter Four

*I*t was hours before I got the chance to speak to Shona. We didn't manage to catch a moment on our own, with everyone crowding around in groups to talk about Neptune's visit all throughout lunch and then having to sit in silence for the ocean studies test.

At the end of the day, we swam out through the tunnels with Althea and Marina.

"That was easy!" Marina said as soon as we were out of earshot of the classroom.

"What did you put for number four?" Althea asked.

"Angelfish," Marina replied quickly.

"Yeah, me too."

Shona was busy stroking the glittery gold starfish she'd won for best outfit.

"So swish, Neptune coming to *our* school," Althea murmured.

"I know," Shona replied dreamily.

"I wonder if he'll get all his treasure back," Marina added, and the three of them talked about his visit all the way to the end of the tunnel, where Shona and I said good-bye to the others.

As soon as they were out of sight, Shona turned to me, her eyes almost popping out with excitement. "So? What were you trying to tell me this morning?" she asked. "Was it about the ring? Did you really lose it?"

I glanced around before replying. Some younger merchildren were laughing and playing in the sea on their way home from school. A couple of them had caught a ride home on a dolphin. Others were chasing one another or jumping over waves. The sun beat down on us.

I pulled Shona into a rocky crevice. We swam between the rocks, taking a long route home. Once I was sure there was no one around, I pulled my hand out of my pocket. It slid out easily this time. Twisting the ring around so she could see the diamond, I held my hand out.

"Swirling sea horses!" Shona said, swimming up

to look more closely. "You had it all along! But why did you say you'd lost it?"

I wondered whether to tell her the truth about the weird feeling I'd been getting from it all day. How crazy would it sound, though? And was it a good idea to involve her at all? Last time I'd dragged her into one of my adventures, it had nearly wrecked things between us. But could I really go through this on my own?

"You promise not to tell anyone about this?" I asked, deciding our friendship was strong enough.

Shona looked at me blankly. "Why? Why the big secret? How come you didn't turn it in, Emily?"

I shook my head. "I couldn't."

"'Didn't want to,' you mean?" Shona said. "Emily, you heard what Mr. Beeston said. Neptune will be furious if anyone—"

"I *couldn't,* Shona," I said more firmly.

She stopped and stared at me. "Why not? What do you mean?"

I looked up at her from under my eyelids. I could feel my tail quiver as I blushed. "You'll think I'm crazy," I said.

"Of course I won't," Shona said, laughing. "I *know* you're crazy. Come on, it's me, your best friend. Tell me!"

I smiled, despite my weird feelings about it all. "OK." And before I could talk myself out of it, I found myself telling Shona all the things I'd been feeling since I'd been wearing the ring and about my hand getting stuck in my pocket while Neptune was at school.

"It was so strange, when I was looking for it. I had such a strong feeling, as if it *wanted* me to find it," I said.

I stopped talking and waited for Shona to speak. This was where she would tell me I'd completely lost it and she didn't want to be my friend anymore. Why had I risked her friendship again? Was it too late to take it all back, say I was joking?

I stared down at a skinny sea horse bobbing along the seabed, its bright orange color standing out against the white sand. A shoal of butter hamlets drifted by, taking no notice of the sea horse or of us.

Finally I looked up at Shona. She was staring into my face. "You promise you're not making this up?" she asked.

"Of course I'm not making it up! Why would I want you to think I'm even nuttier than you already do?"

"It must be magic, then," she said, her eyes shining with delight. "It's so beautiful," she added with a touch of envy. "Can I try it on?"

I laughed. I might have known Shona would want to try it for herself.

I tried to pull it off my finger, but it was stuck. I pulled harder—and a rushing noise flooded into my head. Thundering and rolling. What was it? There was a storm raging out at sea. I could feel it. Waves crashing everywhere, thunder booming into every corner of the sky, lightning cracking the world open. And grief. I wanted to cry. Wanted to break down in floods of tears and cry till I'd filled an ocean. I squeezed my eyes shut, stopped trying to pull the ring off, and clasped my hands over my ears.

Instantly the storm stopped.

"What was *that*?" I asked.

"What?" Shona looked bemused.

"The storms, the sea crashing."

"I don't know what you mean," Shona said. "I didn't feel anything." She looked at me sideways for a second, then shook her head and examined the ring again. I flicked my tail to stay upright and still as she stared at it. Was she joking with me? How could she not have noticed the storms? "It's really the swishiest thing I've ever seen," Shona breathed, staring at the ring as though it were the only thing in the world.

"I can't get it off," I said.

"Here, let me try." Shona reached out and I held my hand open for her. But the second she touched the ring, she catapulted away from me as though she'd been shot out of a cannon, landing in a bunch of mossy seaweed.

I swam over to her and pulled her out. "You all right?" I asked.

"It burned me!" she shrieked, pointing at the ring. "Or bit me, or something!"

I yanked at the ring again. "Don't be silly. It's just—"

"I don't want to try it! You keep it. It's fine." Shona dusted her tail down, wiping sand and moss from her scales.

I twisted the ring back around on my finger so the diamond could stay hidden against my palm. I felt safer with it that way.

"Come on," Shona said. "Let's go back to your place and do our homework."

She swam off without another word.

I knew as soon as we reached *Fortuna* that something was wrong. The first person I saw was Millie. Not that that was so unusual. She often came over to see Mom.

But she was on her own, sunning herself on the front deck. If "sunning herself" is the right expression. Millie must be the only person in the world who manages to sunbathe in a long black gown. She never wears anything else. She'd pulled it up to her knees and was stretched out on a blanket, a packet of cards spread out in a star shape next to her.

"Where's Mom?" I called as we approached the boat.

Millie looked over and squinted into the sunlight. Sitting up and pulling her gown back down to her feet, she shuffled the cards into a pile. Shona and I swam up to the side of the boat. "She had to go out," Millie said in the mysterious way in which she says everything.

"*Had* to? Why? Where?"

"She just—look, it's not really for me to explain."

"Fine, I'll ask Dad."

I swam to the front of the boat and was about to dive down to the porthole when Millie said, "He's gone out too."

I stopped, treading water with my tail. "They've gone out together?" I asked hopefully, knowing even before she spoke what the answer was going to be.

"No." She refused to meet my eyes. "No, they've gone out separately. Your mom asked me to wait here for you. I thought perhaps we could play canasta, or I'll do your tarot cards for you, if you like."

"They've had an argument, haven't they?" I asked.

Millie still wouldn't look at me. She started dealing out the cards for a game of patience. "I really think you need to talk to your parents about it," she said awkwardly. "I just don't think it's my place to—"

"It doesn't matter," I said, cutting her off. "Come on, Shona, let's go inside."

We swam silently through the porthole into the downstairs floor of the boat, the part that was filled with water, where Dad lived. I knew exactly what Millie was telling me or, rather, what she wasn't telling me. It was obvious they'd had an argument. They'd been heading in that direction for days.

I'd managed to push the morning's fight out of my mind for most of the day, what with everything else that had been going on. But now, well, that was it. They'd walked out. On each other, and on me too. Was it because of me? If they didn't have to argue about how to bring up their daughter, everything would probably be fine between them.

I know, I know. Overactive imagination again. I was probably blowing it out of proportion. But what if I wasn't? I just couldn't stop the questions from pushing everything else out of my mind. What if they really were going to separate? What if neither of them ever came back?

Shona tried to humor me out of my mood by making silly faces behind the fern curtains and offering to share the bottle of glitter she'd brought home from school. But it was no good. Nothing could lift the heaviness of my mood or the dark cloud of my thoughts.

Mom and Dad were going to split up, and it was all my fault.

"Emily, are you down there?" Millie called from the kitchen.

I raced up to the little trapdoor. Maybe she wanted to tell me Mom and Dad had come home! "Are they back?" I asked.

"I—I'm sorry, dear," Millie said. "I was just thinking I'd make us a snack. I thought you might be hungry."

I suddenly felt empty, but not from hunger.

"No, thanks," I said sullenly, and slipped back down without waiting for her to reply. I twisted the ring back around and studied the diamond, as if it could make me feel better.

Shona was busy painting swirly patterns on her tail with scale polish. She looked up as I swam back toward her.

And then it happened. The shaking, the rocking, waves rolling over one another; even the boat seemed to be moving. Water sploshed in from the trapdoor above us.

"What's going on?" Shona shouted, smearing the swirly patterns into a smudge down her tail.

"I don't know!" I called back, half relieved that at least I wasn't imagining it this time. "Hold on to the porthole!"

We swam as hard as we could to get to the front end, where the large open porthole seemed like the steadiest thing to hold on to. Gripping the sides of it, our tails flailing out all over the place, we waited for the shaking to stop.

"Are you all right down there, girls?" Millie's voice warbled from upstairs.

"We're fine!" I yelled back. "Hold on to the rails, Millie!"

"I am!" she replied. "I'm fine. It'll be all right, don't worry," she added, her voice wobbling with fear. "I'll take care of you!"

Though we gripped the sides tightly, our bodies were flung from side to side, our tails hitting the wall as the boat rocked and shook. It was like an underwater roller coaster ride! Up, down, thwacking us all around, the motion slapped our bodies backward and forward in the water so violently I was nearly sick.

And then it stopped. Just like that. The boat stopped rocking. Shona and I looked at each other for a moment as we became still. Just for a second.

In that second, a sharp pain stabbed my hand.

The ring! It was digging into my finger! *Aargh!* I curled my hand into a ball, the diamond tight inside my fist. Catching my breath, I looked up to see a dark shadow fall over the porthole.

Something was outside. Something big. And it was heading toward the boat.

Chapter Five

"I might have KNOWN!" The voice boomed into the boat like an explosion.

Surely this couldn't be real. Neptune! He was outside the boat, his chariot gleaming in the sunlight, dolphins surrounding him as he raised his trident. The sea around him bubbled like burning lava.

"Come HERE!" he bellowed.

I looked around, desperately hoping I'd spot who it was that he was addressing. I mean, it couldn't be me. It *couldn't* be. What had I done *this* time? Surely this wasn't about the ring!

"Yes," he growled in a quieter voice that was even more threatening than a shout. "You." He pointed directly at me.

I swam through the porthole that we used as the underwater door, my tail shaking so much I thought it would fall off.

"Alone!" Neptune barked as Shona approached the porthole behind me.

"I'll wait here. You'll be OK," Shona whispered, sounding as if she believed it about as much as I did.

I wobbled toward Neptune like a jellyfish and waited for him to speak.

But he didn't. He just stared. Stared and stared at me until I wondered if he was going to turn me to stone with his eyes. But he wasn't even looking into my eyes. He was looking at my open hand, at the diamond.

"For once, Beeston did well," he said in a quiet voice. Quiet for Neptune, anyway. It still vibrated through the air, splashing water across the sides of his chariot with each word. "All those years and it was right here," he murmured even more quietly, his eyes still fixed on the ring.

My hand burned under his gaze. It felt as though it were on fire, flames scorching through my fingers, screaming along my arm, into my body, all through me. I clenched my teeth and waited.

Eventually, Neptune raised his head to look me

in the eyes. "Remove it," he said simply, holding out his hand.

"I—"

"The ring. Give it to me. NOW!"

As he waited for me to hand over the ring, the sea rocked and ebbed around us. I bobbed around, bouncing up and down in the water while I fumbled and pulled at my finger. My hands shook with terror. I couldn't do it. The ring was completely stuck. My finger swelled and throbbed.

"I—I can't," I stammered, my words jamming through the thudding in my mouth.

At this, Neptune rose higher in his chariot. As he did, the waves grew sharper, splashing against me, slapping my face, pulling me under. "Come here," he said. Swirling my tail around as hard as I could, I propelled myself back up and swam toward the chariot.

Neptune held his trident in front of me. "Put your hand out," he said. I did what he said. Then he reached toward me with the trident and touched the ring.

The result was electric. Literally. I felt as if I'd been struck by lightning. My body zipped into life as though a thousand volts were buzzing through every nerve. Neptune must have been struck too. His beard seemed to have flames flying from it. His tail was shooting sparks out in every direction. A jagged orange light danced and crackled between us, alive and on fire.

Neptune finally pulled the trident away. Breathless, he paused to gather himself. Then he reached out with his hand. Grabbing my wrist, he pulled at the ring.

"AAARRRGGH!" he screamed, leaping backward. He shook his hand, blew on it, plunged it into the water. As he did so, the sea raged around us, building into the worst storm I'd ever seen. Clouds darkened, blackening the sky, closing down on us. I was being tossed around everywhere. Even *Fortuna* shook so violently that it was starting to break free from the spot in the seabed where it had been deeply stuck for more than two hundred years. The boat heeled madly from side to side.

"Damn those vows!" Neptune bellowed. "They were not meant to prevent *me* from touching the rings! I am the king of all the oceans!"

What did he mean? What vows? Why couldn't he touch the ring?

As if he'd heard me, Neptune snapped his head around to face me. "That ring has been out of my sight for hundreds of years," he said. "And that is exactly where it should have stayed. Never have I thought of it in all those years. Never. Not once did I question its whereabouts." He laughed sardonically. He wasn't smiling, though. "Although

I should have known the kraken would have found it and protected it. The kraken understands loyalty."

Neptune looked up to the sky. "It should have remained hidden, out of sight, buried in the seabed," he called to the clouds, which split apart and cracked in claps of thunder. "I need it to be buried, along with everything it represents."

Then he turned to me. "You have brought back to life what should have remained forever out of mind, forever forgotten," he said. "Get out of my sight."

I didn't need to be told twice. I swam as hard as I could toward *Fortuna*.

I could see Millie, gripping the rail with both hands, her legs thrown from side to side on the deck, her black gown whirling out around her. Shona must have still been inside. Plowing through the water as hard as I could, sinking with every stroke, plummeting down and swirling around before being thrown back above the water and landing again with a splash, eventually I made it to the boat. I gripped a lower railing and tried to steady myself.

"No! Wait!" Neptune called to me. "I will not allow this to happen!" A streak of lightning zigzagged across the sky, ripping it in two. The boat swayed again, dragging me under the water and hurling me back up. Gasping for breath, I clung to the porthole as thunder exploded across the sky. It sounded as though someone were beating a bass drum with speakers the size of a planet.

Neptune's face had turned purple. "You cannot defy me!" he barked. "I am Neptune, king of all the oceans, and you will NOT take advantage of my laws. Do you hear me?"

I nodded frantically. "Yes, Your Majesty," I said, my voice shaking. "I hear you. I—I'm sorry. I didn't mean to steal your possessions. Please, I'll give it back. I'll put it back exactly where I took it from." I struggled with the ring. Again, it wouldn't budge. My finger felt bruised.

But there was part of me that was glad it wouldn't come off. The ring made me feel—what was it? Safe. Important. However strange it made me feel at times, the strongest sensations I got from it were ones that made me feel comforted and protected.

"Enough!" Neptune boomed. "I WILL have it back. And I know how to get it."

"What do you mean?" I asked, gripping the side of the boat as it swayed in the waves that were still crashing all around us. "I don't understand what I've *done*!"

"It's what your parents did in creating you!" Neptune bellowed. "And now I shall *un*create that."

Uncreate me? What did that mean? I swallowed hard through a throat that felt as if it were filled with a giant rock.

Neptune paused for a moment and looked away. When his eyes returned to bear down on me, I thought there were tears in them. Neptune, crying? If I weren't so terrified, I might almost have laughed. The thought was ridiculous. Neptune didn't cry!

He slowly raised his trident. As he held it above his head, the waves increased, the sky darkened even more, *Fortuna* rocked to the side. "YOU!" he boomed over the cacophony of the raging storm. "You shall no longer be semi-mer. You shall not have the privilege of living both on land and in the sea. You shall NOT share my world with any other."

"What do you mean?" I cried. "I don't understand!"

"THIS is what I mean!" And then he waved his trident above his head, swirling it around and around. As he bellowed his curse at me, the sky began to swirl too. A dark cone of clouds spun across the horizon, skating toward us, whipping up the sea in its wake, gathering pace, growing in size, and darkening in color with every second.

"No longer may you be a semi-mer. You will be one or you will be the other."

"No!" I shrieked. "Which will I be? Do I have to decide?"

"You do not CHOOSE! You do not have a say. It is *my* choice, your fate. Mer or human—*I* will decide, in *my* time. And here is where the curse begins."

Another wave of the trident; another black cone spinning toward us, this time drilling into the sea. I clung more tightly to *Fortuna,* trying as hard as I could to pull myself into the boat.

"You will know the curse is upon you as soon as I finish speaking," said Neptune. "You will feel its effects begin. In a matter of days, when the moon is full, the curse will be complete. And you shall take your new form."

My new form?

"In the meantime, as the curse unfolds, you will gradually lose aspects of both your human and your mer self. While you are human, remnants of your mermaid self will remain, and while you are mer, the human half will still be felt. Until one sides takes over completely, you will be neither one nor the other."

In that moment, I lost the ability to fight back, to argue, even to believe there was anything I could do. There was a tiny split second when everything became calm. The sea, the sky, even the air around me—it just stopped. Stopped dead. Like my thoughts.

"Emily!"

Someone was calling me from the boat. Millie! I'd forgotten about her! She was still on the deck, soaked and bedraggled. Her hair was plastered all over her face; her gown stuck to her like an extra skin. "Emily! Get inside—quick!" she yelled.

Without thinking, I darted through the porthole—just in time. A second later, Neptune howled, "I will NOT be cheated. I WILL NOT forgive. I am NEPTUNE, the ruler of ALL the oceans, and my rule is the LAW!"

And then it struck us. All I saw was blackness, whirling blackness, surrounding us. Then the tornado wrapped itself around the boat, drilling into the sea and sending us spinning.

I couldn't hear Neptune's words anymore, but I could still sense his rage, still feel him shouting to the sky as *Fortuna* was raised and hurled in a million directions.

It seemed to last forever. It was like the scariest ride you could ever imagine at a fairground, the fastest, most dangerous roller coaster in the world—multiplied by a thousand. I clung to one of the benches that stretched across the lower level of the boat. I tried to scream for Shona, but I couldn't even use my voice. My words were whipped away from me as soon as I tried. Was she still there? All I could see was water whirling around and around, a cyclone even within the boat. Side to side, back and forth like a rodeo horse, we tipped and spun and clattered. I tried to scream, but again and again the water snatched away my words, my gasps, even my thoughts.

In the end I just hung on. I twisted the ring around, clutched it in my palm, and prayed that the cyclone would soon stop—and that I would still be alive when it did.

Eventually the cyclone slowed. It felt as though we'd been in the storm for hours and hours. It was stopping. The boat still rocked and dipped, still turned uncontrollably, but there were calm moments in between. It was in one of these calm moments that I finally managed to call for Shona.

"Emily?" Her voice, from somewhere at the opposite end of the boat, was the most welcome sound in the world.

"Shona!" I called again. "Where are you?"

She emerged from under the table that used to have all Dad's things on it. I shook away the pain that stabbed at my chest when I thought of him.

Shona looked as I've never seen her look in my life, and as I don't think she'd ever want anyone to see her again. The blond hair that she spent an hour a day brushing was matted and splayed across her face; the glittery patterns she'd been painting on her scales all day had run and splattered into dark, smudgy patches all over her tail. Her face was so white it was almost transparent. She looked like a ghost. A mermaid ghost.

As she swam toward me, I could tell by the expression in her eyes that I probably looked just as bad. At any other time, we would have laughed. I'm sure we would have. But laughter seemed as out of reach as every other normal thing in my life. We fell into a hug.

"What happened?" Shona asked in a numb voice.

I shook my head. "I have no idea. Neptune—he was angry. So angry."

"I told you what his anger could do, didn't I?" Shona said. "I told you it could create storms!"

"Well, yeah, ages ago—but I thought that was just stories, things you learned in your history lessons. I didn't think we could actually be caught up in one!"

"No," she said, "nor did I." She looked out through the porthole. "At least it seems to be stopping," she said hopefully.

Just then, Millie shouted down through a trapdoor. "Emily, are you all right?" she called, her voice coming out in gulps. "Oh, Emily, please answer me. Are you there?"

I swam over to the trapdoor. "Millie, I'm fine! And so's Shona."

"Oh, thank the goddess, thank the lord, thank you, thank you!" Millie sobbed. "Oh, if anything had happened to you, I just don't know what I— oh, Emily, I'm so sorry."

"It's not *your* fault!" I said, reaching up to pull myself through the trapdoor. Millie was sitting on the floor shaking, surrounded by the contents of our home, scattered all around her. Clothes were strewn all over the floor. Drawers were hanging open; glasses and dishes were smashed to pieces everywhere. I could hardly bear to look.

I hitched myself up and sat on the floor with her. My tail flapped and wriggled as it began to fade away. Starting from the tip and working all the way up, I felt it turn numb, then gradually fade away as my legs reemerged, tickling like a nerve recovering from a local anesthetic.

"Come on, Millie. It'll be OK," I said, reaching out to put an arm around her. I have no idea what made me say that. Perhaps I hoped that Millie would believe me and then she could convince me it was true.

Her big shoulders heaved and shook; her head bowed as I tried to comfort her.

As I sat awkwardly patting Millie's shoulders, I waited for my tail to finish transforming. But something wasn't right. It seemed to be taking longer than usual. My legs were fine. A bit numb, a bit tingly, but they looked normal enough. It was my feet. They weren't forming properly. *Come on. What's the matter?* It didn't usually take this long. My toes still seemed to be joined together, kind of webbed.

Webbed? A cold dart of terror stabbed at my ribs. Neptune's words. *You will be neither one nor the other.*

The curse had begun.

"Emily, Millie, I think you need to look outside." I didn't have time to dwell on my thoughts any longer. Shona had swum over to the trapdoor and was pointing urgently out through a porthole. "Go up on deck," she said. "I'll swim around and meet you."

I stood and helped Millie to her feet, and we stumbled together out onto the deck, picking our way through the debris that lay everywhere. I tried not to focus on the strange sick feeling stirring in my stomach as I walked across the deck with feet like rubber.

I don't know what I expected to see outside the boat. Don't know if I thought that somehow it would all look the same as before, now that the storm had passed. Or if there was a part of my brain clinging to the crazy hope that we were somehow still at Allpoints Island.

But if I had thought anything of the sort, I was in for the biggest disappointment of my life.

75

I didn't recognize anything. I could hardly *see* anything, for that matter. Just sea. And sky. No island. No other boats, no bay. And not another soul in sight.

There was a stillness in the air as though the world were holding its breath, waiting till it was sure that the storm had really passed.

At first, all I could see was the ocean, deep navy blue, lying still all around us, still as a hundred miles of glass. Just above it, a low mist hovered in a perfect line.

The sun was beginning to set, the sky bruised with clouds like bunches of deep mauve cotton, stealing whatever bits of blue they could find. Wispy gray mists floated higher up, racing the slow, heavy clouds below them.

Then the edges of the clouds began to change and brighten as though someone had taken out a peach-colored felt-tip pen and was drawing an outline around each one. As though they wanted to make up for the heavy blackness of the storm. Soon pink and orange seeped into the spaces between the clouds. The sun forked out, through every gap it could find, in bright orange fans. It was like a painting.

A lone seagull sailed across the sky as though it were putting its signature on the picture.

And then we saw it.

"Look," Shona whispered. She pointed into the mist along the horizon. Millie and I peered to follow the line of her finger. Gradually it came into view as we stared, standing out above the mist as though it were balancing on it.

A castle.

Chapter Six

"Where are we?" I whispered.

No one replied.

We went on staring, each thinking our own thoughts and silently asking our own questions. I didn't ask any more questions out loud. What was the point?

Standing at the very front of the boat, I slowly turned around in a circle, taking in the whole view. Absolutely the same all around us. Totally, totally still sea. Stiller than I had ever known it, bluer than

I had ever seen it, quieter than I had ever heard it. The boat lay on the slightest tilt, lodged on something. But what? There was no land to be seen, nothing to be seen at all, in fact, except the ocean, and the castle, and the mist.

Shona ducked under and swam out of sight. A moment later, she emerged, wiping the hair from her face. "We're stuck on a sandbank," she said flatly.

A sandbank. In the middle of the ocean?

Shona shrugged and shook her head in answer to my unasked question.

I squinted at the castle to examine it more closely. It stood proud and majestic above the sea: a gothic silhouette against the sunset, like a cardboard cutout. It was a child's picture of a castle, perfectly symmetrical, a turret balanced squarely on each side, a tower in the center. Two thin arched windows were just visible in the top corners. As I looked, something tugged at me. It felt as though there were a wire between the castle and my chest, pulling at me. I knew in that moment I would have to go there.

The sky was turning red behind the castle, blacking out everything except its outline and the line of mist wafting around it like cigar smoke. Every now and then, as the mist ebbed and flowed, I noticed that the castle seemed to be standing on an island of rocks. Jagged and threatening, they held it high, as though carrying it on a platform, a grand stage in the middle of the ocean.

Millie was the first to shake herself out of the trance we all seemed to be in.

"All right, girls," she said, dusting herself off and shaking out her gown. "I'm going to find out where we are." As soon as she spoke, the feeling about getting to the castle left me as rapidly as it had come.

Shona looked blankly up at her from the sea, as though Millie had spoken in a foreign language.

"How?" I asked.

Millie gave me a big false smile. Just like the ones Mom gives me when she doesn't have a clue how to work something out either. "I'll find a way. We'll have you back with your mom and dad in no time. Just you wait," she said, doing nothing to soothe my worries. If anything, she'd made them even bigger. Who said Mom and Dad *wanted* me back? Maybe they'd both realize they were better off without me messing things up all the time. Millie looked down at Shona and gave her one of the not-real smiles too. "You too, dear. I'll work something out. Don't worry."

She stepped carefully across the deck and patted the big, long sail that lay rolled up along the side. "Come on, let's see if we can get this up," she said. "We could sail back, no problem."

I stared at her in disbelief, briefly shaken from my somber thoughts. Surely she didn't really believe we could sail *Fortuna*?

But then I thought again. Why not? Perhaps we could! If only we could figure out where we were, maybe we could get it started and sail back to Allpoints Island. I mean, sure, it was an ancient pirate ship that had been wrecked on the reef two hundred years ago and hadn't been sailed ever since. But we weren't exactly overwhelmed with other options. What harm could it do to try?

Together we pulled and tugged at the ropes and poles, Millie heaving the boom high enough for me to dodge underneath, the sail in my hands. Around and around I went, unwrapping the maroon fabric until it lay across the whole deck. I tried hard to ignore the rubbery feeling in my toes, pushing it away like all the other horrible things I was trying not to think about.

"Oh," Millie said, looking down at the torn, fraying, useless sail at our feet.

I looked down at it with her. "Maybe we could sew it?" I said eventually.

Millie sighed and smiled tightly. "We'll give it a try, dear," she said, patting my arm. Neither of us mentioned the fact that the boat was stuck on a sandbank and that the lower half of it was submerged in water. Or the fact that we didn't happen to have the tiniest idea of where we were. We needed something to cling to, even if it was a complete illusion.

"We'll work something out," Millie said as she

turned to go back inside the boat. "Now I'll just have a cup of Earl Grey, and then what do you say we get started on the cleaning up?"

We managed to put everything back where it belonged. Everything that wasn't completely smashed to smithereens, that is.

The worst part was when I came across a glass that Dad had given Mom only a couple of weeks ago. He'd painted a heart with their initials on the side. It was broken right across the middle of the heart, their initials on separate shards of glass at opposite ends of the boat. It wasn't significant, I told myself again and again. It didn't mean anything. I wasn't superstitious.

But I couldn't convince myself. It was all I could do to hold back the tears lining up behind my eyes, desperately trying to squeeze out.

It wouldn't have been so bad if I hadn't seen Millie suck in her breath between her teeth and shake her head when she saw it. As soon as she spotted me, she did the smiling thing again. "It's only a glass," she said. "We'll get your mom a new one, soon as we get back, eh?"

Then she ruffled my hair and sent me off to the kitchen area with a brush and dustpan.

It was pitch-black outside by the time we'd finished. I went downstairs to see Shona while Millie made us all a snack. She'd figured out that if we rationed ourselves tightly enough, we could survive for a week on the food and water we had on the boat. "Not that we'll be here anything like that long," she'd said brightly. "But just so's we know."

Shona and I talked about what had happened, going over it again and again, trying to make sense of it.

"So, he tried to get the ring from you, but he couldn't even touch it?" she asked for the fifth time. "But Neptune can do anything! Why couldn't he get it back if he wanted it so much?"

"I don't know," I said, as I'd said each time we came around to this point. "He said something about his own law stopping him."

Then I paused. I hadn't mentioned the curse yet. I didn't know how to. So far, the worst effects had been while I was human. What would happen as my merself got worse? Or what if that was the half of me I was to lose forever? If I wasn't going to be a mermaid any longer, that would mean I'd lose Shona as well as everything else that was going to happen. I'd never be able to go out swimming in the sea with her again. I might have one of Neptune's memory drugs forced on me and never even remember her! My best friend, the best friend I'd ever had.

And there was the other thing too. The thing that was so awful, I kept trying to stop myself from even thinking the words. But they were there, in the center of everything. *My parents.* Was I ever going to see them again? If I lost half of what I was, did that mean I would lose one of them as well? Even if they wanted to be together, maybe it wouldn't be possible. The thought was like a kick to my stomach.

"Shona, there's another thing," I said nervously. "A really bad thing."

So I told her about the curse, about how it would take a few days to work, and I wouldn't know which way it would go, but whichever way it did, that was where I would stick. I stopped short of telling her it had already started, about how my feet hadn't completely formed when I was on the deck. And how even now, swimming down here as a mermaid, I could feel something was different. Just here and there a scale missing. Bits of flesh showing through my tail. She didn't need to see that yet, the proof that the curse had already started.

"Fighting fins!" Shona exclaimed when I'd finished. "That's awful! What are we going to do?"

"That's what I thought you'd help me work out."

Shona grabbed my hands. "I will, Emily," she promised. "We'll stop this from happening, OK? As sure as sharks have teeth, I'm not going to lose you.

Whatever happens. And you're not going to lose your parents either."

I winced at her words as though she'd lashed me with a piece of wire. Just the thought of it!

"We're going to solve this, all right? You and me, we can do anything, can't we?" Shona looked at me desperately, her eyes begging me to say yes.

I looked at her and squeezed her hands. "Of course we'll solve it," I said, lying as much as she was lying to me with her words, and as much as Millie had lied with her smile. "Of course we will."

I stood on the front deck with Millie. Shona was in the water next to the boat. I rubbed my stomach, trying to ignore the fact that it was rumbling from my rationed dinner of a third of a can of beans and a piece of toast. A feeling of warmth spread into me from the ring, against my body. Everything was going to be OK. I could feel it. The ring was telling me so.

"That's the Plow, and that's Orion's Belt," Millie said, pointing up at the stars, clustered together in tight clumps. I craned my neck to follow the outline she was pointing out. I don't know how she could tell what was what. The longer I stared, the more it just looked like a completely black sky filled with a million billion tiny white dots.

"What's that?" I asked, pointing to a dark shape like a shadow in the distance. It was coming closer, changing as it slid across the sky. Another cyclone? Please, no!

It looked like a giant snake, gathering and bunching up into an arc, then stretching out to form a long black line cutting through the stars. It was heading for the castle. The shape disappeared into the mist, reemerging above it to swirl around the top of the castle, circling it, spinning into a spiral, around and around, tighter and tighter, faster and faster, until it faded into nothing. It was one of the strangest things I'd ever seen. And one of the most magical too.

We stared into the black night. The shape didn't come back.

"I have no idea," Millie said eventually. "I've never seen anything like it in my life. And I'm not one for superstition, as you know, but I'll bet it's portentous. Let me think."

"What about the stars, though?" Shona asked. "There are constellations that can help us work out where we are, I'm sure of it. I just can't remember what they're called. Or what they look like."

Which was a big help.

"I've got it!" Millie said, her eyes brightening. "I have a great idea." She headed back inside the boat and beckoned me to follow.

For a moment, for one silly, ridiculous, heart-stopping moment, I actually thought she'd come up with a plan to get us out of this. I let myself hope. Until she said, "I'll do our tarot cards."

I followed Millie into the kitchen. "You clear a spot for us, and I'll lay out the cards," she said.

Shona swam up to the trapdoor as I pushed a couple of chairs to the side. She poked her head through, and I sat on the floor by the trapdoor to join her. Then Millie came in with the cards and we watched intently as she shuffled, spread the cards in a six-pointed star, and slowly turned them over one by one. She didn't speak, didn't explain anything. When they were all faceup, she sat looking at them for ages, nodding slowly.

"What do they say?" Shona asked.

"Do they say anything about my mom and dad?" I asked.

"Or mine?" Shona added quietly. That was the first time I had really thought about her parents. She'd been taken away from them too. They wouldn't have a clue what had happened to her. They hadn't seen her since she went to school that morning. I'd been so selfishly wrapped up in my own problems, I hadn't thought about Shona's.

Would anyone tell them anything back at Allpoints Island? What would happen when Mom and Dad came home—assuming they ever did—and found that *Fortuna* wasn't even there? Would they come after us? Would they know where to look? They'd find out, wouldn't they? But what if they didn't? Suppose they didn't come home at all! Suppose they'd had such a big fight, they'd split up and both forgotten all about me!

No! I couldn't let myself think like that. I couldn't! Surely they'd do something. They'd get together with Shona's parents and send out a search party or something.

They'll find us. They'll find us. They'll find us. I repeated the phrase over and over and over like a mantra. *Please let me believe it,* I added.

The cards didn't tell us anything. Anything beyond what they normally said when Millie read anyone's tarot cards. We had a long journey ahead and the outcome was uncertain. A tall, skinny stranger with jet-black hair would help guide us, the truth would elude us, and all would be well in the end. Blah, blah. Why I ever put faith in Millie's card reading, I don't know. It was about as useful as trying to tell the time from examining your freckles.

"Look, let's all try and get some sleep," she said, shuffling the cards away when it was clear they hadn't impressed either of us or helped us find an answer to any of the questions we weren't saying out loud. "Things are bound to look better in the morning, once we've had a few hours' nap—and perhaps a cup or two of Earl Grey."

I stifled a laugh. Admittedly, a slightly hysterical one. It was really pretty hard to see how things were going to look better. But she had a point about the sleep thing. I was exhausted.

"Shona, you take Jake's room," Millie said. "You'll be all right down there, won't you?"

Shona bit her lip and nodded.

"I'll join you if you like," I said softly.

"No, it's OK. I'll be fine."

"I'll be just above you. Knock if you need me."

Shona smiled, although her eyes stayed misty and sad.

"It'll look better in the morning," I said, repeating Millie's lie. It kind of helped to keep saying these things out loud. If we did it often enough, perhaps they'd come true.

"Night-night, you two," Millie said. "I'm going

to get some shut-eye myself now. Although goddess only knows how I'll sleep without my agnus castus tablets."

We each withdrew to our own rooms, our own thoughts, and our own fears.

The moon rose as I lay on my bed. I watched it climb past the porthole. A fat, wonky shape like a slightly deflated ball, it shone down on me, right at me, as though it were personal. Just me and the moon, staring each other down. It was getting fuller every day, every single moment. Racing me to my fate.

The black sky, endless behind it, filled slowly with clouds: some huge and unmoving, like snow-clad hills, others gray and broken-up, like crazy paving. Lighter, wispy clouds sailed slowly in front of them all. And the moon stood firm, almost whole, like a circle drawn freehand by a child. Not quite perfect but not far off.

"Please let this be a dream," I whispered, twisting the ring around and around on my finger, talking to it as though it could hear my thoughts and turn them into reality. Was it a friend or enemy? What was its hold over Neptune—and over me? I couldn't tell.

All I had was the knowledge that it was caught up in this whole nightmare with us—and the tiny feeling that it might help us find our way out of it too.

Please let me be back at Allpoints Island in the morning, I prayed. *Please let me hear Mom and Dad arguing in the kitchen as soon as I wake up. Please.*

Next time I looked, the clouds had all moved on. The stars were no longer visible either. Just the moon remained, bright and proud. *See?* it seemed to snicker at me. *I win.*

There was a split second as I woke up when everything felt normal. Any second now, Mom would call me to get up and I'd have to drag myself out of bed. She hadn't called yet, though. Still half asleep, I stretched and turned over in my warm bed. I was about to go back to my dreams—and then I remembered.

I sat bolt upright, then jumped out of bed and ran to the porthole. *Let me see Allpoints Island. Let us be back there.*

I was greeted by the sight of mauve sea stretching out forever, everywhere I looked. Baby-blue sky. And the white line of mist hovering in the middle, dividing the two worlds.

"Emily, are you up?" Shona's voice called quietly from below.

I ran to the trapdoor and dropped myself down to join her. As soon as my legs touched the water, I felt them change. *Please work properly this time,* I said to myself, and I held my breath as I felt my tail form. Closing my eyes, I focused for a moment on the feeling, willing it to work completely. But it didn't. In fact, it was worse than before. Patches of scales were missing; the shine of my sparkling tail seemed duller; my tail moved more stiffly.

I swallowed my feelings and hoped Shona wouldn't notice. I still didn't want to admit it out loud: I wasn't a mermaid half the time anymore. Now I wasn't even close to being a real mermaid.

"Look." Shona pulled me over to the large porthole door. We swam out through it, around the huge sandbank under the boat, and up to the surface, where we rested, treading water by the side of the boat. Directly ahead of us, hovering on the line of mist as though it were floating, the castle stood bold and gleaming in the sunlight. "I think we should go to it," Shona said, echoing my thoughts from yesterday.

"On the boat? How? You saw the sails."

Shona was shaking her head. "No, I meant just you and me. We could swim there. It doesn't look far."

It was still early. I could tell by how low the sun was in the sky. In fact, now that I looked, I could still see the moon, hanging on like the last guest at a party, reluctant to leave but fading and tired. Could I edge ahead in the battle that was silently taking place between us? Millie would still be in bed. She always slept late. We could get there. As soon as the thought came into my mind, my hand grew hot. The ring—it was telling me something, I was sure of it!

It was telling us to go.

"Come on," I said, feeling hopeful for the first time since we'd landed here. "Let's do it."

Chapter Seven

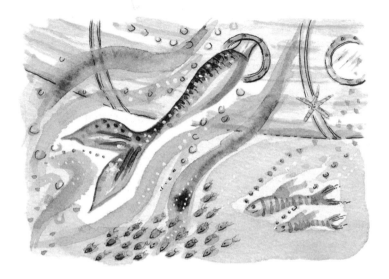

ow long have we been swimming?" I asked, panting to catch up with Shona. Surely she was swimming faster than usual! I could hardly keep up with her.

"Not sure. Maybe twenty minutes, half an hour, tops."

I stopped where we were and flicked my tail around in fast circles to tread water. "Look," I said, pointing to the castle. It seemed to be looking back at me, willing me to approach it. Pulling me along. But there was a problem. A big problem.

Shona looked across at the castle. "What?"

"It's no closer. It looks just as far away as it did from the boat."

"Don't be ridiculous," Shona said with a laugh. "It's just . . ." Then she glanced back to see where we'd come from. *Fortuna* was a dot in the distance. She turned back toward the castle. "But that's . . . but it's not possible."

"It's like a rainbow," I said. "The nearer you get to it, the farther away it seems."

"But how?" Shona's voice broke into a whine. Her eyes moistened as her bottom lip began to tremble. I almost expected her to howl, "I want my mommy!" And why shouldn't she? That was certainly what I wanted to do. I felt like a burst balloon.

"Come on," I said flatly. "Let's go back to the boat. Maybe Millie will have some idea what's going on. You know she thinks more clearly in the morning once she's had a cup of tea."

"Or ten," Shona added with a hint of a smile.

I smiled back. "We'll figure it out," I said. "Don't worry."

As we swam back, I didn't tell her how stiff my tail was getting, how it was starting to feel as if I were dragging a lead weight behind me. Or how that was part of the reason I felt defeated. I pretended I wanted to go more slowly to take in the view: the sea, calm and smooth as we cut through it, the mist lying low and still on its surface.

Eventually we got back to the boat and swam in through the porthole. Almost as soon as we did, Millie's voice warbled down to us. "Emily? Shona? Is that you?" she called, an edge of panic in her voice.

"Hi! We're here!" I called back.

"Oh, thank heavens," Millie breathed, her face appearing at the trapdoor as she leaned over it to look down at us. "Where have you been?"

"We just went out for a quick swim," I said.

"Emily." Millie's tone had turned serious. Her voice a low rumble, she said sternly, "You must never, ever, go out without telling me again. I am responsible for you. I would never forgive myself if anything happened to you. Do you hear me?"

"I'm sorry," I said. "We were just—"

"It doesn't matter now." Millie waved the rest of my sentence away. Just then, I heard a cough from somewhere behind her.

"Who's that?" I blurted out. My heart lifted. Mom and Dad were here after all! They were waiting for the right moment and were going to appear any second, with big smiles, and tell me this had all been a joke, or a mistake, or—

"There's someone to see you," Millie said in a voice as flat and lifeless as a dead eel. And then, cutting my hopes like the sharpest knife, a face appeared next to hers.

Mr. Beeston.

"Hello, girls," he said, squinting down at me and Shona.

"What are you doing here?" I asked through a tight throat. "How did you find us? Where are my parents?"

"Now, now," Mr. Beeston said with a crooked half smile. How could he smile? Didn't he understand anything that was going on? Or was I mistaking him for someone who cared? "One thing at a time. You calm yourself down and then meet me on the front deck." He nodded at Shona. "And you too, child," he said. "You'll all need to hear what I have to say." He pulled back a sleeve of his old nylon suit to glance at his watch. "Let's say ten minutes." And then he was gone.

"I'll be with you," Millie said softly. "I'm not going to leave your side till we've got this settled, all right?"

I nodded. My throat felt too thick and too dry for me to speak.

Mr. Beeston was waiting on the front deck, sitting on a bench and looking around at the horizon.

"Now then," he said as Millie and I sat on the opposite bench. Shona perched on the edge of the deck, her tail draped loosely over the side, flicking the water with tiny splashes. *How much longer will I be able to do that too?* I glanced at my hands. The skin reached up along my fingers now, joining them together, lodging the ring even more tightly in place. What was happening to my body? It was just as Neptune had said. Until the curse was complete, I wouldn't be one thing or another. What did that make me? A nothing?

I couldn't bear to see the evidence, so I stuffed my hands in my jeans pockets and waited for Mr. Beeston to explain what was going on.

He cleared his throat. "Now then," he said again, "you are probably wondering why I'm here."

D'you THINK?

I bit my lip. It was never a good idea to interrupt Mr. Beeston. It only took another half hour for him to get going again. He wasn't a big fan of sarcasm either—or of nerviness. Or of me. So I kept my mouth shut and counted to ten.

"As you know, I was entrusted by Neptune with a most important job. And, as you also know, there had been a certain amount of disturbance, which I was in the process of endeavoring to correct. In fact, even as I speak, some of the folk at Allpoints Island are gathering the final few items of lost treasure. The project has been very successful, largely thanks to your resourceful teacher. All of which helps make Neptune happy. However, as we *all* know . . ." At this point, he looked around at the three of us with one of his crooked smiles, trying to include us, as though we were all in this together. How could we be, when he was the only one who had any idea what was going on?

Again, I stopped myself from saying anything. I counted to twenty this time.

"As we all know," he repeated, "the situation has changed somewhat. Since events took the turn they did, Neptune's attention has wandered from his initial intentions. And so we have found ourselves in this situation."

He folded his hands in his lap.

"What situation?" Millie asked. "I don't have the slightest idea what you are talking about. Now, are you going to explain what in the cosmos is going on here, or am I going to have to—"

"Calm down, calm down." Mr. Beeston waved a hand at her. "I am getting to it."

Then he fixed his eyes on me. "Emily here has found something we never even realized was there, something that Neptune wants back, and perhaps if I tell you a little bit about it, you will understand why. Then maybe we can work together to solve the problem, and all will be well."

"'All will be well'?" I exploded. I couldn't stop myself this time. There weren't enough numbers to count to that would halt my rage. "All well? We're lost out in the middle of the ocean with nothing but sea and mist and a spooky castle that doesn't even seem to exist. Shona's parents haven't seen her since yesterday morning. *My* parents have been arguing and probably never want to see each other or me again—"

"Come on, Emily. You know that's not true," Millie interrupted me.

I ignored her. "And, to top it all off, Neptune's done *this*!" I pulled my hands out of my pockets and held them out in front of me. The skin had reached even farther up my fingers. They were joined at least a third of the way up, lodging the ring so tightly on my finger it hurt.

"Emily!" Shona gasped, edging forward to look more closely at my hands. "What's that?" She looked disgusted. I knew she would.

"I didn't want to tell you," I said. "I didn't know if you'd still want to be my friend if you knew."

"Knew what?"

"The curse. It's already started," I said. "I'm not a real mermaid anymore, or a real girl. I'm nothing."

I felt a couple of tears roll down my cheeks, salty drips running into my mouth.

"Oh, Emily," Millie said. Her voice cracked— with what? Sadness for me or disgust at the sight of my horrible, strange hands? Without thinking, I twisted the ring around, trying to make it feel more comfortable on my finger.

"What in the name of the goddess is that?" Millie suddenly gasped. "And where did you get it?"

Mr. Beeston pulled at his tie. "Millicent, if you will allow me to explain."

Millie waved a hand at him. "Go on. Whatever you've got to say can't make things any worse, I suppose. Just say what you've come to say and get on with it. And then maybe you can go away again and let us figure out what to do next."

"I shall indeed say what I have come to say," he said in that annoying I'm-so-much-more-important-than-you voice of his, "if you will let me."

Mr. Beeston pulled on his tie and flattened down his hair again, and eventually said, "You need to understand the importance of what you have here, Emily."

"What I have where?" I asked. As if I didn't know.

Mr. Beeston pointed at my hand. "There," he said simply. "You see, this ring has lain out of sight, hidden and protected by the kraken, for many years. For generations."

"How can it be so important if it's been buried all that time?" Shona asked. "Why was it buried at all if it's that important?"

"It wasn't. It was discarded."

"Discarded?" Millie burst out. "Who by?"

"By Neptune."

For a moment, we all fell silent. Then, in an even voice, Millie quietly said, "Charles, we would appreciate it if you could stop talking in riddles and please explain what is going *on* here."

"I shall tell you everything!" Mr. Beeston blustered. Then he paused for ages, clasping his hands together and looking out to the still sea that lay waiting silently—like the rest of us. "Many, many years ago, Neptune was in love," he began. "As you know, he loves easily and has many wives, but none like this one. None like Aurora."

"Aurora!" Shona interrupted. "But I've heard of her! She's the human. The one who broke his heart. The one who turned him against intermarriage and everything. We studied it last year in history!"

Mr. Beeston nodded. "Exactly."

I couldn't help holding my breath while I waited for him to continue.

"Aurora was the only wife Neptune truly loved with all his heart. When they married, they had rings made to symbolize their love. One contained a diamond, to represent land. The other held a pearl, to represent the sea. On the day of their marriage, they exchanged these rings. Aurora gave the diamond ring to Neptune. He gave her the pearl."

I touched the diamond as he spoke. I was wearing a ring that was given to Neptune on his wedding day? Given to him by a wife who left him and broke his heart? No wonder he had gone into such a rage! But how was I to know? It wasn't my fault!

No, it wasn't your fault, a voice seemed to echo. Not even in words; it was just a feeling. A feeling of comfort and reassurance—and it was coming from the ring. Twisting it back again to hold the diamond against my palm, I curled my fingers around it, my heartbeat settling as I did so.

"On the day she broke his heart, Neptune took her ring from her and buried it."

"Where?" I asked.

"That I cannot tell you," Mr. Beeston said. "That information is not something you need to have."

He spoke so haughtily I knew it wasn't worth asking again. It would only give him the chance to refuse me again and make himself feel even more self-important than he already did.

But I couldn't help wondering about it. There was another ring similar to mine buried out in the sea somewhere. A ring Mr. Beeston didn't want me to ask about—which in itself meant it was probably important!

"What about his own ring, the diamond one?" Millie asked.

"In his rage, Neptune hurled it with all his might across the oceans. This is the first time it has been seen since that day. No one knows when the kraken found it. All we know is that it did, and it kept it safe and hidden with the many other jewels at Allpoints Island."

"And when the kraken awoke, the ring was disturbed along with the rest of the jewels?" Shona asked.

"Exactly."

"And now Neptune wants it back." I swallowed. "But it won't come off me."

"Why not?" Millie asked.

Mr. Beeston looked down, flattening his jacket and picking off an imaginary speck of dust. His suit was shabby as usual, a button missing on one side, a hole overlooked on the other. "The rings can only be worn by certain folk. Either by a couple in which one is from land and the other is from the sea or by a child of such a couple. It was in the wedding vows between Neptune and Aurora, and the rings were infused with this power. Worn by a semi-mer, this ring cannot be removed."

"Sharks!" Shona breathed.

"So how did he remove their rings in the first place?" Millie asked.

Mr. Beeston sniffed. "The love was dead. The connection was broken."

"That's why he cursed me," I said quietly. "So he can remove the ring."

"Correct. When the moon is full, the spell will be complete. You will no longer be a semi-mer. You will not be able to touch the ring—and it will not be able to touch you. It will fall from you as you would jump from a fire."

"And Neptune can have it back," Shona said.

"He wants it hidden again, along with his memories and his long-buried grief. He cannot exist like this, and if Neptune can't live, none of us can. You yourselves have felt the effect of his current state. It will only get worse. That is what we all have to look forward to if the ring is not buried again. Just more of that and nothing else, for the whole merworld." He turned to me. "Is that what you want, Emily? Is it not an honor to make a sacrifice like this for your king?"

I couldn't speak.

"So why are you here?" Millie asked coldly. "Has he sent you to do his dirty work?"

"Dirty work?" Mr. Beeston spit. "Dirty work? I consider it the highest of honors to be called to duty by my king, to be graciously offered the opportunity to make amends for my earlier failure." He pulled himself up straighter in his seat.

"Like I said, do his dirty work," Millie said under her breath.

"I am responsible for this ring, and I will ensure that it is returned to Neptune. Make no mistake: that is what I will do," Mr. Beeston concluded.

"How did you find us?" I asked numbly.

"The ways of our king are immeasurable. He made it possible for me to be here. That is all I need to know. It is not for you—or me—to question his methods beyond this."

"He's got no idea, is what that means," Millie said. I smiled despite everything.

"I have to go soon," Mr. Beeston said, ignoring

her as he glanced around at the endless ocean, as though waiting for his signal to leave. The ocean responded in the same way as it did to everything else—with silence and stillness. Then he turned to me. "But, Emily, I shall not be far away. I shall be back very soon."

"How will you get back? Can't you let us go with you?" I asked, knowing it was pointless as soon as I'd uttered the words.

"I'm sorry. I have to do as bidden by my king. You will stay here for now."

"How far are we from Allpoints Island?" I asked, edging closer to the questions I really wanted to ask.

"Many hundreds of miles."

I nodded. Another kick, this time in my chest. Finally I said, "And what about Mom and Dad? Where are they? Do they know what's happened? Are they going to come after us? Will they find us too?" The questions ran out in a rush. My heart banged in my ears like thunder while I waited for his reply.

Mr. Beeston puffed out his chest. "Your parents do not know your whereabouts," he said in that Oh-I'm-*so*-important voice again.

"Where are they?" I asked, holding back my anger.

"Your mother is staying on the old boat."

"On *King*?" Millie asked.

He nodded.

"Does she know what's happened?" I asked.

"She knows only that you have been called upon to assist Neptune in a grave matter."

"Has she looked for me?" My throat was full of knives.

Mr. Beeston lowered his head. "She has, yes. We've told her you're not at the island. The other islanders will take care of her, and I am close at hand to support both your mother and Shona's parents."

"And Dad?" I asked. "Where's he staying?"

Mr. Beeston at least had the decency to look slightly uncomfortable this time as he looked at me. What did he see in my face? A reminder that every word he uttered was crashing into my world like a sledgehammer? "I'm afraid they have been separated," he mumbled. "He is staying with Archieval for now."

Archie was another of Neptune's helpers, and my dad's friend. *At least they both have people around them who care, not just slimeballs like Mr. Beeston,* I told myself, desperately grasping at anything that might provide a grain of comfort.

"Why have they been separated?" I asked, my breath catching, and tripping over my words. "Did they choose it themselves?"

"Neptune has decided to go back to the old ways."

"What old ways?" Shona asked.

"He's banned intermarriage again. For good this time. He says he has had enough of the trouble it causes." Mr. Beeston looked me in the eyes. "Your parents are forbidden to be together again," he said dryly.

And that was it. The end of my world. With those simple words. Game over. My insides turned cold and hardened. At that moment, I believe I could have broken into a thousand pieces.

In a matter of days, I would no longer be a mermaid. Or I'd be a mermaid and would never again be able to live on land. And my parents would never see each other again. With a feeling of utter horror, I realized that my worst fears had come true: I couldn't have both parents. Whether they wanted to be together or not was no longer an issue. They couldn't be together—which meant I could never, ever, live with them both again.

"No!" I begged. I pulled on Mr. Beeston's arm. "Please, no!" Tears slid down my face. *"Please,"* I begged. "You have to make Neptune change his mind. You have to do something. Please!"

"There is nothing that will change his mind," Mr. Beeston said, his voice steady and cold. "Neptune's word is law. Your parents will come together one last time when Neptune brings them to you. Under the full moon, when the curse is complete, you will have a chance to say good-bye to one parent. You will go home with the other."

"No!" I fell to my knees in front of him. I hated myself for begging to Mr. Beeston, of all people. But it couldn't happen. It *couldn't* happen. It couldn't.

But as Mr. Beeston shook me away and dived off the side of the boat, disappearing deep down into the sea, I knew the truth. It was going to happen. It really, really, was. The changes I was feeling now were only a forerunner to the real curse, which would take place under the full moon. One half of me would triumph; the other would be gone forever. And there wasn't a single thing I could do to stop it.

Chapter Eight

*A*ll right, that settles it," Millie said, blowing on a cup of tea. "I'm not letting you out of my sight. If Neptune can send Mr. Beeston here from nowhere, who knows what might happen if you went out there?" She cocked her head to point out at the endless ocean. "You could be kidnapped and taken away forever." She shuddered. Then she reached out to pat my knee. "You're my responsibility now, dear," she said gently, "and I'm going to take care of you."

True to her word, she didn't leave us alone after that. Which meant that Shona and I didn't get another chance to try to swim to the castle, or even talk about it.

The day passed in a blur of Earl Grey, beans on toast, and several games of canasta. I moved along through it as though I were walking through fog. And in a way I was. The mist all around us seemed to have totally clouded my thoughts. Or perhaps it had more to do with the fact that the whole world as I knew it was collapsing around me. The sadness Mr. Beeston had left me with felt like a physical weight dragging me down.

The night wasn't much better. It was filled with dreams about my parents and about the castle. In one, I was swimming toward it as hard as I could. Mom and Dad were waiting for me there, but it kept getting farther and farther away. With every stroke, it became more distant, but it was calling me, willing me to find a way to get there. All around me, voices were urging me on. Then the ring on my finger turned into a knife and cut through the sea so that I could walk there—but I had no feet. My tail flapped lifelessly on the ground for a moment, till the ring shone a beam that lifted me and carried me toward the castle. I almost reached it—it was inches away. And then I woke up.

Panting and sweating, I got up and looked out through my porthole. Directly ahead of me, the castle loomed just as it had in my dream, the mist flowing around its middle like a skirt. Its windows were black, and closed like sleeping eyes. But as I stared, they seemed to brighten, shining at me, just at me. Blinking and glinting, it was as though they were spelling something out in a code I had yet to crack. I knew one thing for certain, though. I had to get to the castle.

It was early, too early for anyone else to be up. Even the sun hadn't risen yet. The sky was a deep purple. I crept out onto the deck and looked around. In the distance, the castle was almost hidden by the mist. Just the turrets were visible, reaching upward, tall and dark and forbidding.

As I looked across, my chest burned. The ring was tight on my finger, the diamond smooth and bright. *What is it?* I asked silently. *What do you want?*

The ring didn't reply. Well, no, it was a ring. But as I closed my fingers around it and breathed in the salty air, I knew I had to try again. My dream had been telling me that there was something waiting for me at the castle. I just knew it. The thought was too strong for me to ignore. I had to get there, and I had to go now. If I waited any longer, Millie would be up, and there was no way she was going to let me out of her sight again. And it wasn't fair to keep dragging Shona off on my crazy stunts. I'd already gotten her into enough trouble. No, let her sleep.

I slipped into the water as quietly as I could. The sea rippled around me as my legs jerked and twitched, stiffening, sticking together, and finally stretching out to form my tail. What there was of it. Again, patches were missing all over. Fleshy white bits of my legs poked through the scales. As I moved, my tail felt taut and tight. It didn't bend right. It was getting worse.

Never mind. Just get there. Determination drove me on, and I ducked my head under the water and swam.

But it was just like last time, and just like my dream. The more I swam, the farther away the castle seemed to be.

I plowed through the water as hard as I could, thrashing my tail with every bit of energy I had, stretching my arms as wide as they would reach, pushing myself farther and faster with every stroke. But it was useless. I was getting nowhere.

Below me, the sea looked dark and unwelcoming.

Jagged rocks were piled on top of each other as though they had been dumped there and forgotten long ago. Small pockets of sandy seabed were dotted about in between. Tiny black fish darted away as I swam across them. A round yellow fish slid slowly in and out of the crevices like a submarine.

I came to the surface to catch my breath. I didn't seem to be able to stay under water as long as usual. That must be the curse too. Where would this end?

No, I couldn't think about that or I'd end up giving up altogether. I couldn't think about anything. I just had to get to the castle. But it was as far away as ever.

As I flicked my tail to tread water, I looked at the ring. "What do I do?" I said. And this time, it did reply. Not with words, but with a feeling, the way it had before. A feeling that seeped through me like heat filling my bones. A feeling of trust. I had to trust the ring. Just like in my dream, if I gave in and let it guide me, it would get me to the castle.

So I did. I stopped trying. I stopped swimming, stopped pushing myself to get there faster or sooner—and instead I listened to the ring. It felt as though I were tuning a radio: finding the right station and getting it clear and sharp.

I held my hand out in front of me, letting the ring guide me. Immediately the water became smoother; a gentle current started to glide me along. With the slightest, tiniest flicks of my tail, I zoomed forward. Heading toward the castle.

At last, it was coming closer! Soon the current slowed. The water seemed to grow thicker, and colder, and much darker.

Below me, a shoal of silver fish swirled down like a light beam, flashing briefly through the black sea. In their wake, a group of manta rays slowly flapped their long capes as they slithered by. I kept well out of the way, watching from behind a rock till they'd passed.

Ahead of me, the sea looked even blacker. As I got closer, I could see a big dark hole, a tunnel. Sharp rocks formed a ring around its entrance.

The strangest fish seemed to pace across the tunnel's entrance, gliding heavily and slowly. Five or six of them. I knew what these were. I'd never seen one in real life, but we'd studied them in Aquatics and Animals: humphead parrot fish. Almost twice as big as me, they looked like big, burly bouncers wearing silly masks and rubber shields. Their bodies were gray, with a purple splotch of paint in a line up their heads like war paint. These fish had jaws you didn't want to get in the way of. Each time one of them passed the tunnel's entrance, it opened its enormous mouth and took a bite at the rock, dissolving it into soft sand. A tiny beach lay around the entrance.

My tail shook. The castle lay beyond this tunnel.
I knew it.

I waited for ages, counting the seconds in between
each sweep of the tunnel's entrance until I'd
worked out the best time to go. One more parrot
fish passed the entrance—and then it was open.
This was it. They were all facing away, swimming
to opposite sides. Any second now, one of them
would turn and swim back. It was now or never.
And never wasn't an option.

So I darted into the tunnel.

It was so cold in there, and so dark. And I felt so
alone. Every now and then, I passed something.
Thin black fish swam in single file along the sides
of the tunnel, coming from behind and overtaking
me. Thick, chunky silvery-blue fish flopped by in
pairs, swimming toward me and sailing over my
head. Trails of seaweed hung from the walls, waving
with the current and making me jump when they
brushed against me.

I swam on.

The tunnel twisted and writhed about like a
giant snake. *Around the next corner, around the next
corner,* I said to myself again and again. It had to end
sometime.

And then it did.

The tunnel led upward, growing lighter and warmer with every stroke until I emerged, panting and breathless, in a round pool. I took a few seconds to catch my breath as I glanced around. Where was I?

I swam all around the edges of the pool. The walls were gray rock and covered in green algae; chunks of bubbly seaweed hung down into the water like bunches of grapes on a vine.

Above the water, the pool was enclosed by walls. Gray, lumpy, dark, and cold, dripping with dampness, it was like a long-forgotten cellar, with a metal door in one corner.

I'd done it. I was in the castle. In a cellar. On my own.

What was I *doing*?

I shivered as I pulled myself out of the water and waited on the side, watching my tail flicker halfheartedly, flapping on the surface of the water as it faded away. My legs slowly emerged, numb and tingling. This time the numbness in my feet didn't go away. I looked down. Webbed. Even more so, like my hands.

I didn't have time to think about that, or about any of the fears I could so easily have thought about if I gave myself half a chance. Just one question remained: why was I so sure the castle offered me something? I tried to bat that question away with the rest of my dark thoughts. Whatever the castle wanted with me, I had to find out and get back to the boat. The others would be up soon.

Edging around to the doorway, I felt for a handle. A brass knob turned slowly, creaking like an ancient floorboard as I twisted it. Despite the creaking, it turned easily enough, and I opened the door.

I inched my way up a spiral staircase, gripping a rope handrail for support. Around and around, the stairs climbed steeply and tightly. I felt as though I were climbing into the clouds, floating upward. By the time I reached the top, I was dizzy and disoriented. Another door. This time I held my breath and turned the knob as slowly and gently as I could.

I was in a corridor, wide and long, with pictures all along the walls. Battle scenes, shipwrecks, storms at sea; the kind of thing you always see in castles like this.

I almost laughed at myself. *Castles like this?* How could I even think for a moment that this was like anywhere I'd ever been?

I mean, yes, from the inside it looked a little like

the kind of place you might see in a book or on a documentary or something. But there was something different about it too. Aside from the fact that it seemed to float on a mist in the middle of the ocean, something about it felt unreal—like a film set or a cartoon. I couldn't put my finger on it, exactly, but it was just a tiny step removed from reality. As I moved along the corridor, I felt a little like an actor in a film where everything else is computer-generated animation. Unreal.

I kept glancing at the pictures to see if anything had changed while I wasn't looking—whether the boats had moved or the storms had raged. They hadn't. Of course they hadn't. I was imagining it. I must be.

I crept on down the corridor. Ahead of me, another door lay open. I went in.

It was a smallish, box-shaped room, jam-packed from floor to ceiling with dusty books in fancy bindings, all bronze and gold. The titles were full of words I could hardly read. Most were foreign; a few were English. All looked hundreds of years old. Not exactly your light bedtime reading.

Then I noticed the window. A large rectangle that covered half of one side of the room, it was set into a recess with a small bench. I sat on the bench and looked out. The sea stretched for miles and miles, all the way to the horizon, just as it did from *Fortuna*. But down below, waves lapped on rocks that were gradually surfacing like bared teeth as the tide edged out. It was as though the castle stood on a podium above the rest of the world, separate from the world, floating above it as though in a dream. *What was this place?*

Another door took me out of the library into a smaller room. One side of the room was filled with weapons. Opposite, the wall was covered in silk banners painted with flags from all over the world. I recognized some of the shapes and colors from geography lessons back in Brightport. Others were completely unfamiliar. There was even a skull and crossbones on one flag.

I moved on quickly. The room led out to another corridor. More paintings on the walls, this time portraits. Men in naval uniforms, beautiful women smiling up at them, young men standing proud on the decks of warships, girls perched on rocks. I moved closer to examine the pictures in more detail. *Hold on.* Were they girls, or were they—

What was that?

A bell clanged loudly, echoing down the corridor.

I glanced furtively around. Was it me? Had I tripped an alarm? Was someone going to come out and catch me? *No! Please don't let me be captured again!* Memories of being caught and imprisoned in an underwater cell after I'd awoken the kraken rushed through me with a horrible shudder. I couldn't get caught here!

There was a recess behind me, a heavy wooden door at the back of it. I jammed myself into it, my heart almost bursting out of my mouth. Pinning my body to the door, I held my breath, shut my eyes tight, and prayed for the alarm to stop.

And then it did. Stopped dead. Silence all along the long corridor. Nothing moved.

My body sagged in relief as I leaned against the door, letting out a long breath and trying to decide what to do next.

The relief didn't last long. A moment later, I heard footsteps. They were coming from behind the door, getting closer! There was no time to hide. My body froze as I stood in the recess.

And then the door opened.

Chapter Nine

I was looking into a pair of very green and very surprised eyes.

"Who are you?" asked the boy, staring back at me. He was tall, taller than me anyway, and skinny like me too. He was probably about the same age, maybe a little older, and dressed in black flared trousers and a black T-shirt. He had long jet–black hair parted perfectly in the middle and the most piercing green eyes I'd ever seen, which he continued to fix on me.

For a brief second, I remembered Millie's prediction about a tall, skinny stranger. Was this him? What had she said about him? I couldn't remember. I tended not to listen carefully to Millie's fortune-telling. For once, I wished I had.

"I—I—" was all I managed to say.

The boy glanced quickly down the corridor before beckoning me into the room. "You'd better come in," he said, recovering more quickly than me. His voice was silky and smooth, like his hair, and serious, like his face.

As I followed him into the room, I forced myself to speak. "I'm Emily," I said. I couldn't think of anything else to say. I looked awkwardly around me. Three of the walls were covered with maps and scrolls. There wasn't a blank inch. Every country and every ocean in the world must have been on these walls. The fourth wall had a long rectangular window that looked out to sea. Beneath it, a thick wooden bookcase held rows and rows of books, brown and bound in gold like the ones in the library. The room felt almost unreal, as though the books and maps were part of a stage set and underneath them lay a thousand years of history and mystery.

The boy noticed me looking. "They're from my ancestors," he explained.

"Your ancestors?"

"Pirates, captains, travelers of all kinds," he said.

"Many ships have been wrecked on the rocks of Half Light Castle."

I nodded as though I understood.

"Look, sit down," he said, gesturing to a huge armchair. With its thick, dark wooden arms and green velvet seat, it reminded me of the furniture in the stately homes I'd seen in some of Mom's books. Mom. Just the thought of her made me ache. Where was she now? Was she trying to find me? Would I ever see her again? Each question was like a knife twisting around and around in my chest.

The boy went on staring at me as I sat down. He pulled up an identical chair and sat opposite me. "I'm Aaron," he said. He held out a skinny arm to shake my hand but almost instantly changed his mind and pulled it away.

We fell silent. I didn't have the first idea what to say. Well, come on. How many times do you think about what you'd do if you swam to a spooky castle floating on a mist in the middle of the ocean and accidentally landed in some strange boy's room?

Exactly.

He was the first to pull himself out of the shocked silence. In fact, now that I thought about it, he was more mysterious and cool than shocked. Perhaps he was used to strange things happening. Or perhaps he was just a mysterious and cool kind of boy. Either way, I was intrigued—and thrown off balance—by him as much as by everything else that had happened in the last couple of days.

"How did you get here?" he asked.

"Um, I swam," I said uncertainly.

His eyes opened even wider. "You swam?"

I nodded. "Through tunnels. But where am I? What kind of a place is this?"

"Half Light Castle. It's my home," said Aaron. "I don't know any other."

"You've lived here all your life?"

He nodded. "All my life. Here and nowhere else, like every generation before me, all the way back to . . ." He looked up at me through his thick black eyelashes. "No, I can't tell you that."

"Can't tell me what?"

"My family history," he replied with a grimace. "It's not exactly straightforward. You'll never believe me."

I laughed. "You think *your* family history is hard to believe. Wait till you hear mine!"

He didn't smile. "Trust me. It's complicated. Or it was. There's nothing too complicated now, though, as it's just Mother and me."

"Just the two of you in this whole place?"

"And a few si—" He stopped himself, covering whatever he was about to say with a cough.

"A few what?" I asked.

"Servants," he said quickly.

"You weren't going to say that. What were you going to say?" I insisted.

Aaron shook his head and stood up. "I don't think I can tell you," he said. "I'm not sure. Look, why don't you tell me about you instead? How *did* you get here? It's supposed to be impossible."

"It nearly was," I said. "I tried again and again." Could I tell him about the ring? It was tight on my finger, the diamond warm against my closed palm. I could feel it almost scorching my hand, getting hotter. What was it saying? Tell him? Or keep it to myself?

Why should I keep it secret, anyway? I had nothing to hide. "Look, if I tell you, you promise you'll believe me?" I wanted to tell him. I felt I could trust him. I don't know why. There was just something about him that I could connect with. As though we spoke the same language.

"Why would I do otherwise? Why would you lie?"

"OK," I said. "Well, it was this. It kind of led me here." I held my hand out and opened my palm to reveal the ring. "Now, I know you'll think I'm making it up or you'll think I'm crazy or something, but I promise I'm telling you the—"

"Where did you get that?" Aaron reached out and grabbed my hand, pulling it toward him to look closer. His voice shook so much I could barely understand what he'd said. He swallowed hard, catching his breath. His pale face had turned even paler. "Where did you get it?" he repeated.

"I—I found it," I said uncertainly.

"Do you know what it is?" he asked.

"Well, I—yes, I think I do." Did he know what the ring was? Had he heard of Neptune, heard the story?

"I've never seen it," he said in a whisper. "Not the real one!"

He fell silent, squeezing his mouth into a tight line and his eyes into slits while he thought. "All right," he said, making up his mind about something. "We've got time. Come with me."

With that, he motioned to me to follow him to the door. Glancing down the corridor again, he nodded back to me. "Come on," he said. "I want to show you something."

Aaron led me down a maze of corridors, scurrying quickly along till we came to a thick wooden door with bars and bolts across it. I followed him outside. Below us, the sea washed against rocks in the semidarkness. We ran around to the front of the castle and back inside through a small arched door. Following Aaron inside, I felt as though I were stepping further and further into a dream. Was any of this real? I mean, it *felt* real. The bricks of the castle were thick and hard, the rocks below were jagged and cold. But, still, something in the atmosphere made me feel as though I were floating, suspended just above reality, as if the castle really were floating on the mist.

I closed the door behind me.

We were in what looked like a small church. A tiny chapel in a remote wing of the castle. A few rows of seats all faced a raised platform at the front. Stained-glass windows were filled with pictures of biblical scenes.

I followed Aaron to the raised platform. Right at the back of it there was a chest. He opened it. "Look," he said, pointing inside.

I peered into it. It contained a glass cabinet and, inside that—two rings. I looked closer at the one on the left, comparing it with the ring on my finger. It was identical!

"But that's—but they're—"

"Imitations," he said. "My great-grandfather made them. From the descriptions, from the stories passed down through generation after generation."

"What stories? What descriptions?" I asked, my head spinning. "Do you mean about Neptune and Aurora?"

"You know?" He gasped. "You know the story?"

"That's all I know," I said. "Please, tell me."

Aaron moved away from the cabinet. "When

Neptune and Aurora married, they cast a spell on their rings. While they were held by a human and merperson who were in love —"

He glanced at me to check that I understood what he meant, to check that we were talking about the same thing. Maybe to check that I didn't think he was ridiculous for believing in mermaids. *I don't only believe in them,* I thought, *I am one!* But I wasn't going to say that. Not yet. Not if it was just a story. Surely boys like him didn't really believe in mermaids. Not that I'd ever met a boy quite like him. I don't know if I'd met *anyone* like him before. All I knew was, I wanted to hear all about whatever he had to say.

I nodded for him to continue.

"As long as the rings were worn by one from land and one from the sea who loved each other, there would always be harmony between the two worlds," he went on. "And there was. For the brief time the marriage lasted, there really was peace between land and sea. No ships were wrecked on rocks; no cargo was stolen; no sirens lured fishermen to their watery graves. Just peace. The two worlds thrived together. It was a magical time."

"And then she left him," I said, remembering what Shona had said about her history lesson.

Aaron's green eyes bore down on me. "She *what?*" he asked angrily.

"She—she left him?" I said more uncertainly. "Didn't she?"

"You know nothing!" he snapped. "Believing in such nonsense. How dare you?"

I pulled at my hair, twisting it around my fingers. "I'm sorry," I said. "I thought she did. I thought she broke his heart. I'm sorry."

"She did not leave him," Aaron said firmly. "She loved him more than anything in the world. I'll tell you what her love for him drove her to do."

I clamped my mouth shut. No more interruptions.

"She loved him so much and believed so strongly in the magic they had created that she attempted the impossible. One night, she decided to show him what she could do out of love for him. You know what she did?"

I shook my head.

"She thought she could swim underwater to his palace. She believed their love was so great, it surpassed the normal laws of her human world. She believed she could become a mermaid. She drowned."

Neither of us spoke for a long time. As we stood in the silence, it felt as though the chapel were the whole world. As though the sea outside the window were there only for us. We were somehow at the center of everything, the center of something so important that—that what? I couldn't tell.

"It was her birthday. She'd wanted to surprise him as her present to him," Aaron went on. "Her own birthday, and she wanted to surprise *him*. They'd only been married two years and a week."

"Go on," I said softly.

"When Neptune found her body, he took the ring from her and—"

"I know this part," I said quickly—even if it wasn't exactly how Mr. Beeston had told it. I had to get it right this time, show Aaron he could trust me. "He tore the pearl ring from her finger and threw away his own ring, the diamond one."

"That's right," Aaron said. "And no one has ever seen the rings—till now." He fell silent.

"The kraken had Neptune's ring," I said. "I found it."

Aaron stepped toward me. "Emily, these rings can only be worn by certain folk."

"I know," I said, swallowing.

"A human and a merperson in love, or a child of such a pair . . ." His voice trailed off, and he looked at me, questioning.

I didn't reply. Finally I nodded.

"I thought as much," Aaron said, suddenly smiling. "You're a semi-mer! You are, aren't you?"

"How did you know?"

"You said you swam here through the tunnels. No human can swim underwater that far. It's impossible." He grinned wider. His whole face changed with his smile; it was like watching a two-dimensional picture come to life. "You found the diamond ring!" he said. "You really found it!"

"Why is that so great?" I asked.

Aaron led me back to the glass cabinet. "Look," he said, pointing to an inscription in black, swirly writing beneath the rings.

I read aloud. "'When the rings touch, they will overrule any act born of hatred or anger. Only love shall reign.'"

I looked up at Aaron. "I don't understand," I said.

"There's a curse," he answered me, his face darkening. "It must be undone. And soon."

"What curse?" I shuddered. Did he know about the curse on me? Surely not—he couldn't!

Aaron brushed my question away with a flick of his hand. "We still need to find the pearl ring, though," he said. "And that's impossible."

"Who says it's impossible? I found this one!" I said, my breath tripping over my words as it raced into my throat.

"The second ring will be much harder to find. The one Neptune ripped from Aurora's finger. He swore it could only be found when it was seen under the light of a full moon. But there was a catch."

"A catch?"

"The ring was buried so deep it has never seen the moon's light. And so it has never been found.

Neptune and Aurora married under a full moon on the spring equinox, at midnight. At that moment, the sea's tide is the lowest it ever gets—and only then is it low enough for the ring to be visible. But those conditions occur only every five hundred years. It's virtually impossible to find it. We'll never stop the curse."

"What curse?" I asked again.

Aaron walked to a small recess. His breath misted the windowpane as he looked out. "After Aurora died, Neptune turned to hatred and anger. There were storms for years. Ships were wrecked at sea. Many fishermen died, many humans perished in the seas, over the years that followed. But even that wasn't enough for Neptune. Even that couldn't take away his rage."

"So what did he do?"

"First he banned any more marriages between humans and merfolk. He swore the two worlds would never again live in harmony."

Well, yes, I knew all about *that*. "And second?" I asked.

"Neptune and Aurora had two children," said Aaron. "A son and a daughter."

"What happened to them?"

"In his grief and sorrow, Neptune cursed them," he went on. "His own children. Each of his own children, and their children, and every generation that followed—every single one of them would die young, and always on Aurora's birthday, as she did. He couldn't forgive her—and because of this, her family would forever be punished."

"His family too," I said.

Aaron nodded. "Their family. And there was another curse placed on them. They would never fit in, never be of one world or the other. They would be not quite human, not quite merperson. Whichever form they took, it would always be held back by remnants of their other form. Every single generation forever would be the same. Do you understand?"

Did I understand? If only he knew how well I understood! It was almost the same as the curse on me! "Aaron. Look!" I thrust my hands in front of his face, opening my fingers so he could see how they were webbed.

"Of course," he said. "I should have noticed before. I was too busy looking at the ring. "You're the same."

I nodded.

"The only way to undo these curses would be to bring the rings together again," said Aaron.

"Because the curses came from hatred and anger," I said, finally understanding the significance of what I had found. We just had to find the other ring, and we could end the curse on his family! And end the curse on me too! I could keep being a semi-mer! I wouldn't have to lose my parents! The thought sent my hopes soaring. Till Aaron spoke again.

"But that will almost certainly never happen," he said. "The chance will come only once every five hundred years."

"When was the marriage?"

"No one knows for sure. The wedding was shrouded in secrecy, protected by Neptune's magic. No one has ever known the exact year it took place. I think it must have been about five hundred years ago, though. It could be more. The moment has probably already passed. So the curses will remain forever, and nothing will ever bring back harmony between land and sea."

Aaron fell back into silence. His words spun around and around in my head. I'd found one ring. Why couldn't we find the other?

"Where was it buried?" I asked suddenly. "The second ring. Where was it buried?"

"Right where she died. Just beyond her home." Aaron ran a hand through his sleek hair.

"Her home?" I asked. I was pretty sure what he was going to say. Pretty sure he wasn't just telling me any old story, someone else's story. I was pretty sure it was his story. That her home was his home, her family his. That was when I realized I was pretty sure of something else too. The reason I felt so comfortable with him and cared so much about what he had to say—it was because he was like me. Caught between two worlds. It was almost as though I'd found a brother.

"Yes," he said. "She lived here at Half Light Castle. In fact, Neptune had the castle built especially for her, for them. A place of magic and beauty and love, where their two worlds came together. And ever since, it's been a symbol of the exact opposite, keeping every generation separate from the rest of the world."

"Completely separate? Don't you ever see anyone else?"

"There has been more life here at different points in the castle's history. But it's never been a happy place since that time. And, with the curses, the family's dwindled more and more over the years. It's just me and Mother now. We have a few visitors who bring us our supplies, but they hardly talk to us."

"Why not?"

"Mostly they're sirens, employed by Neptune. They don't dare go against Neptune's rule. They're all instructed not to talk to us, although there are a few who I'm secretly friends with," Aaron said. "It's a pretty lonely life," he added.

Sirens! That's what he was going to say earlier, when he changed it to *servants.* I knew it! And I was right about Aaron being descended from Neptune and Aurora too! Before I had a chance to say anything, the alarm sounded again, crashing into every bit of space around us, filling my head with noise.

Aaron jumped as though he'd been stung. "Mother," he said. "I forgot!"

"What is it?" I called over the din.

"It's my mother. She's confined to bed. She rings it when she needs me. I didn't go to her earlier. Emily, I have to leave." Aaron hurried to the door. "I don't dare take you with me; the shock will only make her worse."

Outside the chapel, waves crashed against the rocks. The sky was starting to grow light; above the mist, clouds were turning pink, anticipating the day ahead. Cobwebs shone brightly in the door frame: elaborate spiraling mazes in one corner, half-finished scraps and threads dangling loosely in another, gaping and half-empty like derelict houses.

"Quick. Go back to the tunnels. It's the only way. It's too dangerous on the rocks." Aaron led me to the door that would take me back to the cellar. "Down there," he said, opening the door and virtually shoving me inside. "You'll find your way back?"

"Yes, of course."

"Come back soon!" he said urgently. "*Promise* me!"

"I promise," I said.

"Good." He allowed himself a brief smile. "I have to go now." And with that, he closed the door and left me in the darkness.

Chapter Ten

*L*owering myself down, I made my way smoothly back to the cellar and set off for *Fortuna*. Heading back didn't feel half so difficult. The current drew me along. The ring vibrated in my hand, buzzing warmly. It seemed as excited as I was. It was willing me to get back to Shona and tell her everything.

As I swam, I watched the sky changing moment by moment, the clouds growing orange and bright. The sun rose in front of me, shining hard into my eyes as though it were a weapon sent to blind me.

Beneath it, the mist rolled along the top of the sea like a thin layer of snow. *Don't let Millie be up yet,* I said to myself, swimming as hard as I could to get back despite my tail feeling as though it were made of iron and despite my breath coming out in rasps, shorter and shorter with every stroke.

The second I swam through the porthole, Shona was there.

"Where have you *been?*" she whispered fiercely.

"Is Millie up?"

"No." She shook her head. "I couldn't sleep and I was calling you. I figured you must have still been asleep."

"Shona. I got there," I said. "I got to the castle!"

Shona whistled. "Flipping fins! How? What's it like? Did you go inside? Does anyone live there?"

I laughed, holding up my hands to ward off any more questions. "I'll tell you everything," I said. "Just let me get my breath back."

Shona listened in silence to the whole story. When I'd finished, she simply stared at me.

"What?" I asked.

"Emily, you have to find the other ring. It's your only hope!"

"I know—but I can't. It's impossible. No one's seen it for hundreds of years. It's buried too deep. It's not suddenly going to turn up now!"

Shona bowed her head. "We have to find it,

Emily. We have to find a way. We can't give up. There's too much to lose."

"You're telling me!" Shona wasn't even the one with something to lose. I was going to lose the whole of the mermaid world or the whole of my life as I'd known it up until now. Mr. Beeston's words hadn't left my mind for a second. *Neptune's word is law.* I would see my parents on the night of the full moon, one of them for the last time ever. And I didn't even know which one.

"And before you say I have nothing to lose," Shona said, reading my mind as usual, "I do. I've got *you* to lose. And I'm not prepared to let that happen. OK?"

I let myself smile at my best friend. "OK," I said.

We stared out at the castle. It seemed to be staring back at us, the mist curling around its base like a dark blanket, the turrets bright and harsh in the sun, the windows shining like lights.

"We can find it," Shona insisted quietly as she swam toward me and grabbed my hand. "Emily, you can end the curse! You just need to bring the rings back together. You'll change Aaron's life as well!"

The thought made my heart soar. A day ago, I didn't even know he existed; now my fate was inextricably linked to his. "Maybe it'll bring harmony back to sea and land too," I said. Before I could stop myself, I added, "And then Neptune would change his mind, and Mom and Dad could go on being together!"

Then I stopped. How could I be such a fool? My shoulders slumped and I sank lower in the water as I thought about what I was saying. What if Mom and Dad didn't even *want* to be together? The way things had been lately, they would probably be happy with Neptune's new law! And then there was, of course, the fact that the pearl ring was buried so deep it would never be seen.

I was going to lose a parent. It would happen just as Mr. Beeston had told us. When the full moon came, Neptune would bring my parents to me and I would say good-bye to one of them—forever. The thought was so dark and so huge, it felt as if I were falling into it, into the deep chasm that was my future. I stroked the gold band on my finger, pressed the diamond against my palm, looking for comfort, but it felt cold. It had no comfort to offer me.

"Who am I kidding?" I said, my words as heavy as my heart. "We're not going to find the ring. We'll never stop all these terrible things from happening."

"We will NOT give up!" Shona said, swimming around in front of my face and lifting my chin just as Mom does when she forces me to listen. "Do you hear me?" she said sternly. "That is not my best friend talking. The one who explores shipwrecks and caves and breaks into prisons to rescue her dad! We'll find a way. OK?"

I nodded gratefully. "OK," I said. She was right. I couldn't give up. I couldn't just let my life slip away, lose a parent, lose half of myself. Being a mermaid wasn't just something I did for fun. It was part of who I was. We *had* to find the other ring and bring the two together. Then anything born of anger and hatred would end. The curse on me would have to be lifted, and the curse on Aaron and his family too. He could have a completely new life. Perhaps he and his mom could even come to Allpoints Island with us! Yes, we *had* to find the ring. It was as simple as that.

"OK," I said again. "We need to find out when the full moon is. That's how long we have till the curse on me is complete. As soon as the full moon has passed, that's it. I won't be a semi-mer anymore, and Neptune will take back his ring."

"And I may never see you again," Shona said quietly.

We both looked down in silence. Below me, a couple of black-and-yellow striped fish darted into the boat like lovers running away together. They swam off to the other end, leaving the sea fans waving gently behind them.

Just then, a shuffling noise above us made us both glance up. Millie's face appeared at the trapdoor. "Ah, you're awake," she said. "I was just going to make some breakfast. You coming?"

"We'll be right up," I said. Conversation closed—for now.

I munched slowly on my one piece of toast. I had to make the most of it; I wouldn't get anything else till lunchtime, and even then it wouldn't be enough to satisfy the gnawing in my stomach. I didn't know if it was just hunger or the pain of missing my parents so much. Either way it hurt.

Millie sipped her tea. "Not the same without milk," she murmured. "I can't be having too much bergamot." She winced as she put her cup down. "So, what shall we do today?" she asked almost brightly. She sounded as though we were on a package vacation and just had to decide among the pool, the beach, and the trip to see the dolphins. "I thought we might try some dowsing," she added before we had a chance to reply. "It could help us to work out where we are."

"What's dowsing?" I asked.

Millie closed her eyes and drew a heavy breath. Gathering her cloak around her, she held her hands up to her chest. "Dowsing," she said, her voice husky and deep, "is the harnessing of the senses—or, more precisely, of the sixth sense."

"The sixth sense?" Shona asked. "I thought we only had five senses."

"Intuition, my dear," Millie replied, briefly opening an eye to glance at Shona. "The ability to dowse is something I firmly believe to be within us all," she went on. "Most of us do not know a fraction of what we can do. For too many of us, our intuition is ignored, or relegated to some backwater of the mind. But it's there. It's all there." She fell silent, nodding gently as she breathed heavily and slowly.

Her eyes closed, she held her hands out in front of her, palms facing up. "Dowsing is often used to find water, but it can do so much more." She glanced at our blank faces before continuing. "In layman's terms, it is a way of tuning in to sources of spiritual power, harnessing nature's own resources just as the chakras harness the powers within our bodies."

"Mm," I said, not following a word.

After a few more deep breaths, her eyes snapped open and she sat up straight. "OK then," she said, smiling at us both. "We just need a Scrabble set and a coat hanger and we're set." And with that, she got up and went inside.

Shona and I took one look at each other and

burst out laughing. "You'll get used to her," I said. "Just look as though you know what she's talking about and you'll be fine."

"But she's got a point," Shona said.

"What? About the dowsing?"

She shook her head. "The stuff she said about harnessing nature's energy. That's what we need to do."

"'Harnessing nature's energy'?" I said. "You're getting as bad as Millie!"

"Emily, we need to use anything we can think of if we're going to find this ring," Shona said irritably.

Millie had joined us back out on the deck before I had a chance to reply.

"It's the perfect time to do this," Millie said, scattering the Scrabble letters on the deck and bending the wire around into a new shape. "I don't know why I didn't think of it earlier."

"Perfect time?" I asked. "What's perfect about it?" What could she possibly see as being perfect about *anything* right now?

"Magical time," she said with a wink. "Spring equinox sometime around now."

"The spring equinox?" I asked, remembering what Aaron had said. The tide was at its lowest point of the year. A brief spark of hope flickered—but went out almost as fast as it came when I

146

remembered what he'd said next. That there would only be one year when the tide was low enough; and that time had probably already passed. I hardly dared hope for the remote possibility that it could be this year.

"In fact . . ." Millie was saying as she reached into the little bag she always carried on her shoulder. She pulled out a small book. It was bound in black felt, with pink and blue feathers around the edges and *Orphalese Oracle* spelled out in fancy letters along the spine. "If I remember right, this year is even *more* special."

"Even more special?" Shona asked, her voice tight and high. "Why is it even more special?"

"Let me check." Millie looked through her book, licking her thumb and flicking through the pages. "Aha! Yes, that's it." She smiled. "It *is* extra special! This year the full moon and spring equinox are at exactly the same time. The same day. And, my word! Fancy that! The full moon is at the same time as the moon's peak." She glanced at me and, probably noticing my blank face, went on. "When the moon has risen to its highest point in the sky, it will also be at its fullest. Very rare. And—well, I *never!*"

"What?" I asked, my nerves about to crash and splinter.

"The full moon occurs at midnight!"

I swallowed hard. "At *midnight*?" I asked, my voice quivering like a freshly caught fish. "Are you sure?"

"Absolutely!" Millie snapped. She tapped the cover of her book. "Emily, you'd be wise not to doubt the word of the *Orphalese Oracle*. Never been wrong yet, in my experience." She tutted loudly and went back to flicking through the book, squinting and mumbling. "Full moon at midnight on the spring equinox," she muttered. "I bet that doesn't happen often."

Happen *often*? How about once every five hundred years! Aaron was wrong—the year hadn't come and gone at all! This was *it*! This year—the one chance to find the ring!

"Millie, can I see?"

She passed me the book. My hands shook so much that the words started to blur. But I saw all I needed to see. She was right! The full moon was at midnight on the spring equinox! My hands shook so much when I read the next part that I nearly dropped the book. The date!

It was tonight.

I handed the *Orphalese Oracle* back to Millie in silence. I couldn't make any words come out of my throat.

"*Very* interesting," Millie said, oblivious to the change in mood as she smiled at us both. Then she put the book back in her bag and picked up the coat hanger. "Now, let's see about this dowsing."

"That's odd," Millie said, frowning with concentration as she waved her coat hanger over the Scrabble letters.

"What? Has it told you where we are?" I asked, edging closer to watch over her shoulder.

Millie shook her head. "It keeps moving over to you." She glanced at me. "To your hands. As though it wants to tell us something about the ring. Watch. It's telling me there's a strong connection between the ring and . . . hold on. It's spelling something out."

I watched her waggle the coat hanger over the letters. It didn't look as if it was doing anything except twitching and wiggling in her hands.

"Something about a star," Millie mumbled as the coat hanger moved across the letters.

Shona hitched herself higher on the side of the deck. "Stars? Maybe it's telling us to use the stars to find our way back."

"No, it definitely has to do with the ring. A strong link with the ring and—hold on. It's not finished," Millie said, following the coat hanger's progress and reading aloud. "Star l-i—"

"Starlight?" I suggested.

"Could be. Wait." We all watched the coat

hanger intensely as it moved to the letter *n,* then *g,* then *s.* After that, it stopped twitching and lay still in Millie's hands.

"Starlings!" Millie said eventually, pulling a hankie out from her bag and wiping her forehead as she put the coat hanger down.

"Starlings?" I repeated blankly. "What have starlings got to do with anything?"

Why? Why had I gone and done it again? Believed that Millie's so-called psychic intuition might bear any resemblance to anything that made any sense? Why?

"I don't know, dear." Millie said flatly. "It sometimes takes a few attempts to work properly. Needs warming up, you know. Why don't you run along for now, and we'll try it again later?"

Shona and I slunk away and left her to it.

"So much for dowsing!" I said, dropping into the water beside Shona. My tail flickered halfheartedly to life, as weak and limp as the few shreds of hope I still had. The full moon was tonight. If we didn't find the ring, the curse would be fulfilled. By tomorrow I would no longer be a semi-mer, and I would have lost a parent.

"Come on, Em. The tide's going to be at its lowest point in five hundred years tonight!"

"But what if it's still not low enough?" I said. "Or what if we've got it all wrong somehow? The curse will be complete tonight. Neptune will take the ring. It's all over." I couldn't bear it—couldn't even think through to the end of the thought. My future was a black hole, and at midnight I would slip into it.

"You have to believe we can do this," Shona said. Her voice was so full of hope, I couldn't help letting her enthusiasm filter across to me. My heart filled like a tight balloon.

"You're right," I said with new determination. "It's the only chance we're going to get, and we can't afford to miss it. We've got to find that ring—tonight!"

Chapter Eleven

B e careful," Shona whispered as she waved
me off from the porthole. "And good luck."
"You too," I said with a hopeful smile. "See you
soon."

"You're sure you don't want me to come with
you?"

"I'm sure," I said. We'd agreed I had to go
straight back to the castle and tell Aaron the news
about tonight. There was no time to lose. Shona
was going to stay behind and fend Millie off if she
came looking for us. Thankfully, she'd become so

absorbed in her dowsing that she wouldn't notice anything for a while. I wouldn't have long, though. The last thing I wanted was for her to worry about me, on top of everything else. Or to keep a closer eye on me and stop me from going out tonight. That was unthinkable! I'd just have to be careful— and quick.

I swam off in the same direction, listened to the ring in the same way, sneaked into the tunnel, and finally came up in the pool in the castle's cellar. I pulled myself out of the water and sat on the side to get my breath back. Panting and exhausted, I wondered how many more times I'd be able to swim here. My body was getting weaker by the hour. My tail was getting more patchy, my breathing more scratchy. *Just one more day. Please let me hold out for one more day.*

A noise creaked behind me. I leaped to my feet.

"Emily!" It was Aaron! He was still dressed all in black, and his hair was tied back in a sleek ponytail; his face shone pale and clear in the semidarkness of the cellar. His smile was the brightest thing on him. "I've been hanging around here since you left," he said, softly closing the door behind him. "I was hoping you'd come back."

"I said I would." I smiled back, almost surprised at how pleased I was to see him.

Aaron took a step nearer the pool, and that's when I noticed something. His feet—they were webbed. Of course they were. He was descended from Aurora, which meant the curse affected him too. Like me, he was stuck between the two worlds, neither fully one thing nor another. More like me at the moment than ever, as he wasn't quite a semi-mer either. The brief silence that fell between us wasn't awkward. It was the silence between two people who know they understand each other without even using words. It was almost like the way I felt with Shona.

He noticed me looking and shyly held out a hand. "Come on, let me help you out of the pool," he said. This time he didn't snatch his hand away. He held it out palm up, fingers outstretched. Showing me. His hands were webbed too, his fingers joined at the knuckle by the thinnest waferlike stretches of skin. As I reached up to grab his hand, it was as though we were shaking on a deal. We were the same. Whatever happened from here onward, we would succeed or fail together.

We sat on the side of the pool. Aaron stared as my tail melted away and my legs re-formed.

"I can't even do that properly," he said. "My legs stick together and my toes flap about a bit, but that's all." He looked at me wistfully. "Just as it's been for the rest of my family, every generation."

"Aaron, we can change it," I said. "That's what I've come to tell you. Tonight's the spring equinox. And the full moon—it's at midnight!"

Aaron's eyes widened. "Tonight? This is the year? How do you know? The secrecy, the magic!"

I told him about Millie and the *Orphalese Oracle*. I didn't mention the fact that Millie didn't always get it exactly right. She had to be right this time. She *had* to be.

"I don't believe it," Aaron said again and again. "I don't believe it. Every spring equinox since I've known about it, I've hoped and wished. I've even searched for the ring myself and prayed the other one would somehow turn up."

"I can't believe I ended up here," I said, looking at the ring on my finger and smiling. I could feel its warmth smile back at me. "I know I've had a few lucky breaks in my life, among all the crazy stuff! But surely that's about as much of a coincidence as you can get."

Aaron shook his head. "It's not a coincidence at all," he said. "The ring brought you here."

"Brought me to the castle?"

"The rings were meant to be together. When one is worn by a semi-mer, it wants to find the other one. While buried, the rings have no power. But when they are free, they want to be together. They're meant to be together. Its own heart brought you here."

We fell silent, lost in our own thoughts, and maybe in our own hopes. "Now we just have to find the pearl ring," he said after a while.

"Not just find it. We have to find it and bring the two rings together under the full moon. It'll be too late after that. As soon as the full moon's passed, I won't be a semi-mer. I'll lose the ring again."

"And if we fail . . ." Aaron looked away as his voice failed.

"I lose a parent," I said.

"So do I, Emily," he said, his voice hardening.

"Huh?"

Aaron took a breath. "Some years ago, life wasn't too bad here at the castle. Generations before me, it was a busy place. Years of ships wrecked on the rocks meant that occasionally the survivors found their way here. And as I told you, Neptune has always installed sirens and some mermen to keep the castle isolated. So I've always at least had *some* company. Much to Neptune's disgust, there has always been love here too. There has always been marriage, always been a determination to cross the forbidden boundaries."

"Between land and sea?"

Aaron nodded and went on. "But with every generation, it was the same. Just as I told you this morning, each one held the same fate. Each died young. The curse lived on from generation to generation. And still does, all these generations later."

I didn't know what to say. I reached out to touch Aaron's arm.

He looked at my hand on his arm, then looked

up at me. "Father was the son of a ship's captain. He swore he would stop the curse before it affected my mother. No one ever knows exactly which year it will happen—only that it's always on the day of Aurora's birthday." He paused.

"Go on," I prompted.

"There's not much to say. He tried to find the ring, and he failed. He searched and searched out there, but those rocks aren't kind, Emily."

"What happened?"

"He drowned."

"I'm so sorry," I said quietly.

"It was three months ago," he added, and I suddenly thought that must be why he dressed so strangely, all in black. He was in mourning.

He turned back to face me, his eyes shining. "That's why we've got to stop this, Emily. Even if the chances of succeeding are tiny, we have to try. We *have* to. This will be the only chance of our lives, and the only way to stop us both from losing another parent."

"Another parent? But—"

"My mother, Emily," he interrupted. "She's dying. It's Aurora's birthday next week. This is it."

That was when I really understood that this wasn't just about me. It was about life and death. Literally. If we didn't find the ring, Aaron's mom was going to *die* next week, on Aurora's birthday, exactly as her ancestors had. And Aaron would die young too! The thought made something clutch at my chest. "We'll find the ring," I said firmly. "I promise."

Aaron tried to smile, but even though he twitched his mouth up at the corners, his eyes were still the saddest I'd ever seen in my life. "Come on," he said, lowering himself into the water. "I need to show you something I've just discovered. After you left, I went to see Mother, but meeting you got me thinking. I went back to the chapel and dug around a little more. Emily, I found something I'd never noticed before. Come and see it."

I followed him back to the chapel.

"Through here." Aaron guided me to the back of the chapel. At the end of the last row of seats, a few steps led down to a tiny gap just big enough for us both to stand in.

Aaron felt around along the wall. He pushed it firmly and the wall creaked—and moved! A hidden door!

I followed him into a dark box of a room.

I looked around, blinking as my eyes grew accustomed to the darkness. Sunlight seeped in from the smallest gaps in the walls, just enough to see around the room: a small rectangle with a long wooden bench all the way up one side, an arched door opposite.

"I never knew it was here," Aaron said, motioning for me to follow him. "Look, I'll show you something strange."

I stumbled across the dark room, my legs trembling with fatigue but anxiety spurring me on. I kept remembering Millie dowsing on the boat. What if she started to look for me? We had to be quick! I shivered as I followed Aaron to the far end of the room. Cobwebs filled every corner.

A row of paintings lined the wall, just as they lined the corridors all around the castle. "More pictures," I said.

Except that these were different. These weren't portraits, or pictures of battle scenes, and they weren't in frames either. They were murals, painted on the walls.

"It's all I've got. Pictures, books, and maps from all around the world. That's my life. That's my school, my history, everything. But none like these." He pointed to the first picture.

Now that my eyes had grown accustomed to the darkness, I studied the painting. A deep blue sky, a churning sea, and a bright white moon shining down on the castle.

"Who painted them?" I asked.

"I don't know. I bet it was my great-grandfather, though," said Aaron.

"The one who made the rings in the cabinet?"

He nodded. "He was obsessed with the curse, with trying to end it. The men in my family always are. These pictures seem like a clue of some sort."

"They are," I said, not even knowing why. The ring burned on my finger. It was the ring that knew the truth. "They are a clue," I repeated. "I'm sure of it."

"A secret clue, hidden from sight."

"But why would someone want to pass on a message in secret?" I asked. "If he was obsessed, why not tell everyone?"

"The only reason I can think of is so Neptune would never know."

"But why not act on it, do something about it?"

"He probably didn't know what it meant any more than we do. But he knew it meant *something*. Look." Aaron pointed at words scrawled all over the walls, painted around the pictures as though revealing the inner workings of the artist's mind. *Why? What is the significance? How many years?* the words said.

"Someone's been asking all the same questions as we have," I said.

"And clearly had about as many answers as us," Aaron replied flatly, "or else we wouldn't be in this position now."

I stepped forward to study the first painting more closely. It was only then that I noticed the shadows in the sky. The swirling patterns looked familiar. A dark, spinning cone in the sky.

Aaron moved to the next picture and motioned for me to follow. It was similar to the first. The same boiling sea, the sky even darker this time, the moon shining a reflection on the wet rocks like a beam from a flashlight. The swirling shapes were there in the sky again. One looked like a spinning beehive, another like a dark trail from a plane that had been looping the loop.

"There's one more," Aaron said, pointing to the third picture. It showed gray rocks and the base of the castle. The swirling patterns were now just one thick black swarm: a whirlwind, its base at the tips of the rocks, in the center of a shining white circle of light.

"I've seen these shapes!" I blurted out, suddenly realizing that the image had stayed in the back of my mind ever since we'd seen it. "The first night we were here! What are they?"

"I've seen them too. Usually at this time of year. It's birds. They come in the millions."

"At this time of year? The spring equinox? But, Aaron, that's proof! They *must* have something to do with the rings! And your great-grandfather knew it too."

"I think you're right," Aaron said. "But the thing none of us knows is, what are they telling us?"

I wasn't aware of whether he said anything else.

I was too busy staring at the words I'd just noticed among the rest, in capitals and underlined, like a title for the paintings.

My eyes glazed over, cold shivers running like electricity up and down the length of my body as I read the words: *THE STARLINGS.*

Chapter Twelve

I don't know how I got through the rest of the day. Shona and I scurried away every chance we got, to talk about what I had to do and how it was going to work out.

We swam around the lower half of the boat.

"OK, so you have to get to the castle, find the other ring, and bring the two of them together," Shona said, going over the plans for what felt like the twentieth time.

No matter how many times we repeated what I had to do, it wasn't sounding any easier.

"All in the minute that the moon is completely full," I said. "Or it'll be too late. Neptune made his message clear enough. When the moon is full, the curse on me will be complete. I won't be a semimer any longer. And that means I won't even be able to touch the ring. I'll lose it forever." *Along with everything else I care about,* I added silently.

Shona looked at me, holding my eyes with hers. "Let's not think like that," she said.

"I'll lose a parent," I went on, ignoring her.

"Emily, please don't."

"And Aaron will be an orphan."

"Emily!" Shona took me by the shoulders. "Concentrate. We can do this, OK?"

"OK," I said lamely. I didn't believe for a minute that we could. The odds were just stacked so high against us.

The sun had set and the moon was up. This was it. A few more hours and it would be fully risen.

Millie wouldn't leave us alone. She stood on the front deck, pointing out the constellations as the stars appeared, one by one, across the vast sky.

"There's Canis Minor," Millie said, pointing at a clutch of stars that looked pretty much exactly the same as all the others. "And, oh, I think that might be the Corona Borealis." She consulted her book, then looked back up at the sky. "Yes, I think it is," she went on, oblivious to whether anyone was actually listening. "Well, you don't often get the chance to see that," she said.

I smiled politely at her when she called me over, making all the right noises so she'd think I had some idea of what she was going on about. All I actually cared about was how I was going to get away from the boat before the moon was at its peak. We *couldn't* risk telling Millie. She might try to stop us, and there was just too much at stake. I glanced at my watch. Nearly ten o'clock. Two hours. I couldn't even jump over the side and sneak away, as she didn't seem to want to leave me alone, let alone go inside.

I tried feigning huge yawns in the hope it would catch on and make her sleepy.

"Why don't you go to bed if you're tired?" was all she said.

Shaking my head in despair, I went to find Shona.

"What are we going to do?" I asked. "I can't get away while she's out on the deck. We're going to run out of time."

"Why don't you just tell her what you want to do?" Shona asked.

"I can't. She's already said again this evening that she's not going to let me out of her sight. I'm not going to chance it. If only I could hypnotize her or something, like she does to other people."

"Hey," Shona said, a slow smile creeping across her face, "I might just have an idea."

She rummaged around in her schoolbag. "Ta-da!" she said, producing her best B&D hairbrush. The handle was made from brass and was cast in the shape of a sea horse; the bristles were soft and feathery. On the back, there was a mirror surrounded by pink shells.

"A hairbrush?" I said. "Shona, this is no time to worry about how we look! We've only got a couple of hours!"

"I'm not worrying about how I look!" Shona said crossly. "Listen. I've got a plan."

As she explained her idea, I couldn't help smiling too. "Shona, you're amazing," I said. "It might just work."

Millie was only too happy to oblige when I asked if she'd hypnotize me. "It's just—I'm so tired, but I can't get to sleep," I said. "I need something to help me. I think your hypnotism is the only thing powerful enough to do the trick."

She giggled and blushed. "Oh, stop it, sweetie,"

she said. But she flicked her shawl importantly over her shoulder as I followed her into my bedroom.

I glanced at the chair I'd set up for Millie by my bed, hoping she wouldn't move it. It was perfectly positioned, as was the hairbrush on the dressing table. As long as she sat down without moving anything, the mirror should be in exactly the right spot for it to reflect her hypnotism back onto her.

"All right, then," she began, settling herself down in the chair. Perfect! I lay on my bed and half closed my eyes. "As you know, this is a powerful tool, so you may find you sleep even more deeply and soundly than usual," she said. "And you may find your dreams are more intense or elaborate. Don't worry about any of this. All that matters is that you have a good, long rest. Now, make yourself nice and comfy and we'll get started."

I fidgeted around for a moment, trying to act as if I were getting myself comfortable. All I hoped was that I wouldn't get too comfortable and fall asleep.

What if it doesn't work? a voice in my head wouldn't stop asking. I did everything I could to ignore it. It simply *had* to work. There was no alternative.

Moments later, Millie was drawling in a deep, low voice about how tired I was getting. "Imagine you are a feather," she intoned, "falling gradually down to the ground. With each breath, you sway a little bit lower, getting closer and closer to sleep."

I couldn't help yawning. *Don't think about the feather. Don't think about sleep,* I urged myself. *Think about what you have to do. Think about your mom, about your dad, about your one single chance of getting them back together. And of not having to leave half of your identity behind.*

That was all I needed. I was wide awake. And panicking so much it felt as if a high-speed train were racing through my chest.

"You're sleepy," Millie drawled even more slowly, "very . . . sleepy . . ." Her voice was starting to sound as if she were drunk. "In fact, you are so . . . very . . . sleepy . . . that you can't even . . . think . . . anymore." She took a deep breath and yawned a very loud yawn before continuing. "All you want is to go to sleep"—a long pause— "beautiful sleep . . ." An even longer pause. She yawned again. "Peaceful . . . deep . . ."

This time the pause stretched on and on until a brief snort erupted through her nose. I waited a few more moments before daring to open an eye.

I had to clap a hand over my mouth to stop myself from bursting out laughing. Millie lay sprawled across the chair, her legs spread out in front of her, head thrown back, mouth wide open, eyes closed.

I quickly sat up on my bed. Carefully edging past Millie, I crept to the trapdoor in the middle of my floor and lowered myself down.

"We did it!" I whispered excitedly to Shona. "She's completely out."

"Swishy!" Shona grinned. "Come on. Let's go."

We swam to the porthole and listened one more time. Nothing. This was it, then.

"Wait," I said. My tail hadn't finished forming. It was taking longer and longer. My legs had stuck together, but there were hardly any scales. I couldn't feel my legs—but I couldn't feel my tail either. It was as though there were nothing there at all. The whole bottom half of my body felt completely numb.

For a second, I panicked. What was going on? Had I become paralyzed? Maybe I'd never walk *or* swim again!

Eventually my tail formed, what there was of it: bluey-green, shiny scales at the ends, fleshy white skin almost all the way down to my knees. It felt wooden and inflexible, flicking halfheartedly in the water. My breathing was raspy. I don't know if Millie's hypnotism had anything to do with it or if it was just the curse, but by the time we swam out through the porthole, I was so exhausted I could almost have fallen asleep in the water. My mermaid self was disappearing before my eyes—and taking my breath with it. I was becoming more and more of a nothing, more and more of a no one. I didn't fit in anywhere. I wanted to give up and cry.

Shona swam ahead, her tail splashing shiny

droplets that sparkled in the moonlight as she swam gracefully along. Would I ever do that again? Not that I ever swam as gracefully as Shona, anyway. My heart felt as heavy as the rest of me.

"Wait," I called, struggling to catch my breath.

Shona slowed. "We've got to hurry," she said. "We don't have long. The moon'll be at its peak within the hour."

"I know. I'm doing my best. I just . . . can't . . . keep up," I gasped.

Shona swam beside me and took hold of my hand. "Come on, Emily," she said softly. "You can do it. You've got me. We'll do it."

I didn't reply. No point wasting my limited energy talking.

But however hard we swam, the castle didn't get closer.

"Where's the tunnel?" Shona asked.

I shook my head. "No good," I said. "Can't hold my breath. Have to just swim."

I tried to do what I'd done the first time the ring had led me to the tunnel. Tried to let go, listen to the ring. I stroked the gold band as we swam and twisted the ring around so I could see the diamond sparkle and glint on my finger.

It was leading us there. I could feel it, even if I couldn't swim through the tunnel, even if the current was so slight I could have imagined it, even if the castle only seemed to be getting closer an inch at a time. Even if I didn't know how we'd find Aaron—or the ring! We were still getting there, and the ring was doing all it could to help. Maybe it was getting weaker, like me.

Please hold out, I begged silently. *Please get us there.*

We seemed to have been swimming forever.

"I can't do it!" I cried. Tears were starting to slip down my face. "I can't do it."

"Emily, look!" Shona let go of my hand to point ahead. I followed the line of her finger. "The castle!" she said. "We're getting closer!"

She was right. My eyes keen against the darkness, I could see it more clearly than ever. The mist lay across its middle like a belt. Above, three large turrets stood proud, serrated against the deep blue night. Its windows shone as though polished, hiding a thousand secrets behind them.

Below the mist, rocks were emerging by the second. Huge boulders lay dotted about on the stony beach. In between them, jagged rocks were scattered everywhere, like a range of forbidding mountains. Waves thundered against them.

The sight of the castle so close spurred me on. I tried flicking my tail, but it hardly moved. My arms were weakening with every stroke, my tail growing more and more like a plank of heavy wood with every flick.

And then the moon was high in the sky. We'd have maybe twenty or thirty minutes till it was at its peak—and at its fullest. It wasn't long enough.

"We're never going to do it," I said. "We might as well give up."

But before Shona had a chance to reply, a voice called across to us in the darkness. "Emily!"

I peered ahead, scanning the rocks.

"There!" Shona screeched, jabbing a finger at one of the huge, jagged rocks, sharp and pointed as a witch's hat, and just as black. A figure stood halfway up its side. Aaron!

"Emily! Hurry!" he called. "Please hurry!"

I couldn't give up! Of *course* I couldn't. It didn't matter if every single cell in my body wanted to scream with exhaustion. I had to get there.

Shona held tightly on to my hand. "We can do it," she said again and again. "I'm going to get you there." But pulling a dead weight along in the water can't be easy for anyone, and even Shona was starting to get tired. Still the castle lay out of reach.

Come on, come on. We have to get there. Inwardly I urged myself on, screamed instructions and demands, begged, bribed. *Just get there. I'll do anything.*

The moon climbed slowly upward, growing

whiter by the second. Any moment now, the curse would be complete and it would all be over. Neptune would be here to claim his ring—and he'd be bringing my parents so that one of them could say good-bye. My chances of solving all this would be lost forever, along with everything I cared about. Including the chance to help Aaron.

I splashed through the water, clumsy and awkward, like a puppy in a lake. Useless. Useless! The castle seemed to be getting farther away. The moon shone down, its beam like a searchlight across the top of the ocean. I kept my eyes on the water ahead of me, hiding from the shaft of light like a fugitive. If it didn't catch me, maybe we would be safe.

I glanced up at the castle. Still too far. It looked like a cardboard cutout against the night sky. A silhouette, the little figure of Aaron standing on the rocks, waving and calling to us. His voice seemed to be getting fainter.

And then something else.

As I stared, a thick black cloud came from out of nowhere, swirling through the sky like a shoal of black fish, then spreading out, slinking like a snake, twisting, turning, up, down, circling around and around. It looked like a giant swarm of bees.

They moved as one toward me and Shona. As they did, I saw what it was: birds. Instantly they flicked and turned, back toward the castle. In a private dance for us, they weaved with perfect grace and timing around and around the castle, gliding in slow motion as though sliding down the banister of a spiral staircase, then bunching into a black ball again, spinning above the castle.

The dance went on and on as the birds whirled upward in the shape of a genie emerging from his lamp. Then, as one, they spread out and flew toward us in a fan. An enormous flock of tiny black birds passed over our heads, chattering in a million different languages and briefly turning the sky black before they disappeared into the distance.

Seconds later, they were back, coming toward us again; more of them this time, a thick black line of them dividing the sky. They just kept coming and coming, more and more of them, to dance and swirl and break up and re-form around the castle.

"What in the ocean is that?" Shona asked eventually, her voice breathless and tight.

"The starlings!" I said.

"Starlings? Are you sure?" Shona asked.

"Positive."

"But starlings don't fly at night, do they? And certainly not out in the middle of the ocean."

I shook my head. "Look at the sky, Shona." It was brightening by the second as the moon climbed higher and higher. "This is no ordinary night."

"You can say that again," Shona breathed. "What are they doing, though?"

As if to answer her, the birds formed themselves

into a tight, perfect cone. Pointed and sharp at its base, it twisted and whirled toward the rocks, around and around like an electric drill. Hovering over a bunch of rocks right at the water's edge, the cone spun as though boring into the ground. As it did, the ring burned on my finger, heating my hand, filling my body with warmth, seeping into me with emotion. And in that moment, I knew.

I turned to Shona. "They're helping us," I said. "They want us to find the ring."

They must have done it every year. They were connected to the rings somehow, and Aaron's great-grandfather had figured out that much too. But we had more on our side than he'd had. We had the diamond ring. And we had the moon. I glanced up. Higher and higher it climbed.

Suddenly I wasn't tired any longer. "The starlings!" I screamed into the air, jumping to life as though I'd been struck by lightning. "Aaron! Follow the starlings!" That's what the paintings had been telling us. I had no doubts at all now. I pointed at the sky, jabbing my fingers again and again at the birds.

Aaron stared at the black swarm above his head. Then, as though the same flash of lightning had struck him too, he jumped into action. Clambering down the rock, he raced to the edge of the water and fell to his knees, scrabbling in the sand and around the rocks.

The moon edged up another notch, shining so strongly that the sky lightened as it rose. It was almost like daylight. It was nearly there, nearly at the center of the sky. *Please, Aaron, find it, find it.* I watched him scrape at the water's edge, stopping to look up at the starlings, then back to the ground, a new spot, a different position, lifting rocks, tossing them aside, digging into the stony ground. Every time, his hands came back empty.

As Shona and I swam on, the water seemed to turn against us. Waves came from nowhere, splashing our faces, ducking me under. Eddies broke out around us, small whirlpools, bubbles cracking and popping like lava. What was happening?

Shona caught my eye. "It's Neptune," she said, her face white and thin. "He must be on his way."

"Emily!" Aaron screamed to us. He was waving his hands in the air. "Look!" He pointed just below the base of the starlings' cone. It was too far away to see exactly what he was pointing at, but as the moon edged even higher, I saw something glint and gleam just below the rocks he was standing on. As the sea withdrew even farther, it shone brighter. The pearl ring.

We'd found the other ring! We'd really done it! The starlings swarmed around the rocks, their wings purple and green in the bright moonlight, before they separated, the line thinning out as they started to move away. Their job was done.

A spurt of energy drove me on. I had to get there before Neptune. Before the moon reached its peak. Before the curse was complete and it was all too late. Urgent thoughts whipped at my mind like the waves whipped across my face, lashing me, crashing against one another like cymbals. *No, they won't beat me. They won't. We've got the rings. We can do it.* Over and over I repeated the same words.

"Hurry, Emily!" Aaron called as he stepped toward the ring.

And then an enormous wave came from nowhere, washing over me, hurling me down into the sea, where I could no longer swim. I pounded back up to the surface, gasping for air.

As soon as I caught my breath, I scanned the rocks. Huge, frothy waves engulfed the spot where Aaron had been standing only moments earlier.

There was no sign of him.

Where was he? What had happened to him?

"Emily!" Shona called me. She'd been thrown even farther away from me. "Hang on! I'll get you," she cried.

Another set of waves threw me under almost immediately, dunking me again and again, only giving me time to catch the smallest breath in between.

I couldn't keep fighting it. I wasn't going to get there. So near, so near. But it was impossible. I wasn't going to make it.

I cried with all the energy I had left, my tears adding the smallest salty drops into the raging ocean. I stopped trying to swim, stopped trying to fight. "You win!" I screamed at the sky, the moon, at the sea. "I give up!"

It was all over. I'd lost everything. My one chance to keep my parents together and go on living with them both. My life as a semi-mer—all of it, gone, taking Aaron's future with it too.

Chapter Thirteen

*A*s I cried, I looked hopelessly out at the sea all around me. We'd never get out of this alive. I couldn't see Aaron anywhere. Shona had drifted farther away. She was still calling me. "I'll get to you. Just hang on!" she cried.

But I could hardly keep my head above the water. When the waves weren't crashing over my head, I was sinking into huge swells, rising up only to be thrown under again.

Then I slipped down into the biggest swell yet. All I could see on every side of me was a deep blue wall of water. It was like a well, with me at the bottom. Surely this was it. I opened my mouth to pray for my life.

But the wave above me didn't break. As it washed past me, I rose onto another crest. I searched the skyline for Aaron and Shona. Nothing. Where were they? I craned my neck, squinting into the distance.

I scrutinized every wave all the way to the castle, searched every rock. And then I saw it. A boat. A small, green abandoned rowboat, paint peeling from it everywhere, its wood rotting and half burnt.

The thought crashed into my head as hard as the waves: the boat could save us. If only Shona could somehow get it to me. Where was she? I searched the horizon. There! I saw her head! We could do this!

"Emily!" Shona called again.

"The boat! Get the boat!" I cried. My voice was hoarse, screaming over thunderous waves.

"I can't hear you!" Shona yelled back. She was swimming back to me. A wave engulfed me before I could reply.

Gasping, pulling hair off my forehead and choking back seawater in my throat, I called to her. "The boat!" I cried. "There's a boat! Find Aaron. Get him in the boat!" Another wave hit me. I choked as I swallowed a mouthful of salty water.

Shona searched the rocky beach. "That?" she

asked, pointing to the abandoned rowboat. It was half filled with water.

I nodded. "Just do it. It's our only hope."

When Shona reached me she gripped my hand for a second. "Stay here, Emily. Just stay here. You'll be fine. I'll come back for you, OK?" Her voice broke as she looked at me.

"Go," I said. "Hurry."

Shona turned and swam away from me, zooming off at full speed toward the rocky beach, the abandoned boat, the boy I hoped with all my heart was still there somewhere.

I watched the moon climb ever higher. How much time did we have? Minutes? Seconds? Would she find him? Did he have the ring? My head was ready to burst with questions.

I squinted across at the castle, the rocky beach. She'd made it! Shona was at the water's edge, dragging the boat into the water and pulling it along. *Please find Aaron. Please find him.*

"Emily!"

Someone was calling me. Near the rocks.

"Someone! Help me!"

Aaron! I could just see his head bobbing on the waves, his hand high in the air, curled into a fist. "I've got it! I've got it!" he shouted. "Someone help me!"

"Shona!" I yelled with every bit of energy I

could muster. She was edging the boat from the shore. I pointed desperately to Aaron. As she turned to look, he waved his fist again. Instantly, Shona pushed the boat out, swimming across toward him. As she pulled alongside him, he clambered over the side, practically falling into the boat.

Come on, come on. All I could do now was wait here and hope with all my might that they got here before the moon had reached its peak. I looked up. Surely it was nearly there. *Hurry!*

Shona was behind the boat, pushing it along, her tail spinning furiously as the boat dipped and rolled with the waves. It kept disappearing as huge swells moved under it, rolling toward me. Each time it happened, I held my breath, closed my eyes, and prayed that it would appear over the top of the next crest. And each time, thank goodness, it did.

Closer and closer the boat edged toward me, Shona swimming, propelling it along, her tail its only engine, Aaron sitting up in the boat, slipping the ring onto his finger. *Please!* I begged silently for them to reach me soon; my body was weakening with every second. My tail had all but disappeared now. My legs felt as though they were glued together and numb. Only my feet were replaced by the tip of my tail.

My breathing scratched and tore at my lungs. I couldn't hold on much longer like this.

"Emily!" Shona called as I flailed about, desperately trying to stay afloat. They were here!

"You were right!" Aaron called as they edged closer. "The starlings, they pointed right at it. All these years I've seen them. I never knew. We never knew." He leaned out of the boat as they glided toward me. "Grab my hand."

I swam toward them as fast as I could, reaching up with my hand, holding it as high out of the water as I could. We were really going to do it! I smiled as my eyes met Aaron's. His fingers were inches from mine.

And then it hit me. The biggest wave of all. Smashing over my head, almost knocking me out, throwing me down deep under the water, flipping the boat into the air. All I could see was a fountain of froth and bubbles, and sand swirling all around me. I swallowed about a gallon of water; my lungs were on fire.

Pushing with all the strength I had left, I kicked with what remained of my tail, clutching at water with my hands as though I could claw my way through it. Eventually I made it back to the surface. Coughing and spluttering, I knew that was the last time I could do that. Next time I would have no strength left to pull myself up.

"Aaron," I gasped. "Shona!"

They were nowhere to be seen.

And then the sea really erupted, shaking and rocking like the biggest whirlpool in the world. I knew it could mean only one thing: Neptune had arrived.

I saw him in the distance, his chariot pulled swiftly along by about twenty dolphins. They charged toward us. I felt like a prisoner on death row, ready to give up completely.

"Emily!" a voice called behind me. I swiveled around. Aaron! One hand still held high in the air, he was paddling toward me on a piece of driftwood. "The boat collapsed," he gasped. "This is all that's left."

I swam frantically toward him, willing my tail to hold out for just a few more moments.

"The moon," Aaron panted. "We've only got a minute."

A wave washed over my head, but I shook it off. Paddling furiously, I made it to the makeshift raft and grabbed hold of it, gasping for breath. One more minute and then I'd lose the ring forever. Everything that mattered to me would slip down to the bottom of the sea with it, never to be seen again.

I could hear Neptune roaring instructions at the dolphins, waving his trident in the air.

"Now!" I said, holding out my hand. Aaron was wearing the other ring. He held his hand out to mine. The pearl glowed white. The diamond burst with brightness. It was almost blinding. The sea bubbled and boiled all around us as we fumbled to try and bring the two rings together. *Come on, come* on!

Neptune was in front of us, his face as angry as the darkest thunderstorm, his trident high above his head, his eyes burning with rage. And then—

The sea stopped moving.

The mist cleared.

Neptune opened his mouth to yell at us. Our hands met.

And the rings came together.

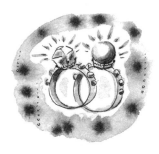

Chapter Fourteen

We'd done it! We'd really, truly, done it.

We held hands with the rings together, each gripping the raft with the other hand. Light fizzed out from them like an exploding box of fireworks: white lights rocketing into the sky, bright blue balls of energy whizzing around and around, orange bubbles exploding all around us. I laughed with relief, tears rolling down my cheeks.

With every spark, I felt the life return to my broken body. My tail burst into action with the light, filling up, flicking the water. My tail had come back! I was still a semi-mer! We'd beaten the curse!

"Look!" Aaron arched his body; something flipped onto the water behind him. A tail! Sleek and black, it shone and glowed as it batted the surface of the sea. "My tail," he said, staring at it in wonder. "I've got a tail!"

"We did it!" I cried, clenching his hand tight as we held the two rings together.

And then Neptune rose in his chariot, his figure blocking out the moon itself.

He opened his mouth to speak, to roar, to do all the things Neptune does. I squeezed my eyes shut in anticipation. What would he say? What would he do now? Surely he wasn't going to leave it like this. How could we have thought for the tiniest second that we could get away with it?

But no sound came. Eventually I opened my eyes again, to see Neptune in the same position, his hand in the air, his body taut and tense, the sea around him motionless. He was staring in our direction, but not at us.

I turned to see what he was looking at. At first I thought it was just the mist, hovering around the castle as it always did, bunching up into a ball. But there was something inside the mist. A person. A woman. She had the most beautiful face I'd ever seen. Eyes as green as the brightest emeralds, framed by thick black lashes. Hair jet-black, stretching down her back. She reached out a hand to Neptune, holding his eyes with hers.

"Aurora?" he said eventually. "Is that really you?"

Aurora? Aaron's ancestor? The woman who broke Neptune's heart?

As she smiled back at him, her eyes brightened even more. Her smile seemed to illuminate the whole ocean. "It's really me."

"How? How are you here?" Neptune's voice grew hard. "Is it magic? A trick of the light? What is it? How do you come before me like this?"

"Every year at the spring equinox, I wait for you. I try to find you. I have never seen you until this time. . . ." She swept a hand in front of us, smiling down at me and Aaron as she did so. It felt like the sun coming out. "This time, the rings have come back together, and they have brought me to you, and you to me."

"But you left me," Neptune replied, his voice even harder. "You broke my heart. You cannot mend it. You can never undo the suffering you caused me!"

Aurora held a slender finger to her mouth. "Don't say this. Never say such a thing. I would never leave you."

"Liar! You did. You left me!"

"I was a mortal. I wished with all my heart not to be. I even tried. For you. And I drowned trying to swim to you. . . ." Her voice was fading.

"But you still left me alone," Neptune called. "Still without you."

The mist swirled around her face, wrapping around her like a scarf. "You must forgive me," she whispered.

"Aurora!" Neptune called. Waving his trident at the sky, he cried, "Don't go! I ORDER you to stay! Do NOT leave me!"

The mist had all but swept her away. Her image. Her spirit. Whatever it was, it had almost faded completely.

"It's after midnight. The moon has passed its peak. We are moving into day, toward the light, the spring, new life. I cannot stay. Forgive me," she said, her voice as gentle as a breeze. "Forgive me. I beg you, forgive me." Again and again she repeated the same words, until there was no more voice, no vision, only the wind, and the moon, and the night.

In the silence, we watched the mist that continued to swirl around the castle, wrapping it in fog. Neptune stared the hardest. His eyes didn't flicker.

Aaron let go of my hand. "Look," he whispered. Under the moon's power, the pull of the rings had loosened. Aaron slipped his from his finger. After putting it carefully on the raft, he held his hands up. In the moonlight, I suddenly realized what he was looking at. The webbing. It was gone.

Gently placing my ring next to his, I examined my own hands. They'd gone back to normal too! I laughed with pleasure, grinning at Aaron, at Shona, at—

"Gotcha!" A hand snapped up out of nowhere, snatching the rings from the raft.

"No!" I lunged forward to grab them back, but it was too late. I dived down into the water. Fueled with new energy, my mermaid self intact, I swam as hard as I could to catch whoever it was who had stolen the rings. But he was too fast for me. He bolted away, swimming like a lightning streak toward Neptune's chariot.

When I came back up to the surface, I saw who it was, smiling his smarmy, creepy, nasty smile, holding out the rings for Neptune to take. Who else?

Mr. Beeston.

"Neptune won't fall for any of that sentimental garbage!" he snarled. "Oh no, he knows what is important in life. What really matters, what—"

"Beeston!" Neptune growled.

Mr. Beeston bowed low, holding the rings out in front of him as he flicked his tail to tread water. "Your Majesty," he said, his voice deep and intense, "I humbly return to you what is rightfully yours. I swore my allegiance to you, and I have not failed you. Finally, the rings are back with you. Once again, they may be parted and buried, safely out of trouble. And, you have my word, I will never, ever, let anything like this happen again." Mr. Beeston went on bowing so low his head was practically under water. No one else moved. No one spoke.

Then Neptune held out a hand. "Give me the rings," he said.

Mr. Beeston instantly swam forward to hand the rings over to Neptune. "Your Majesty, I am humbled by your—"

"Silence!" Neptune barked, his face contorted—with rage, with pain? I couldn't tell.

I stared at him. After everything we'd done, everything that had happened, how could it go wrong so quickly? Now that Neptune had the rings back, he could curse us all over again—and this time there wouldn't be a single thing we could do about it.

I sank lower in the water, my tail hardly moving. Shona swam over to join me. She took hold of my hand. "I'll always be your best friend," she whispered. "Whatever happens."

But maybe she wouldn't have that choice. None of us had any choices anymore. All the choices were in Neptune's hands. Literally.

Neptune flicked his trident in the air. Instantly, three dolphins swam to the side of the chariot. He bent down to say something to them and they disappeared, returning moments later pulling something along. Another chariot, a sleigh of some kind. There were two people in it. A woman and . . . a merman, his tail slung over the side. No!

It couldn't be! But it was. Mom and Dad. Of course! Neptune said he'd bring them tonight!

I swam as hard as I could to reach the boat. "Mom! Dad!" I cried with every tiny bit of me. But the joy I felt disappeared as soon as I saw their faces.

Of course.

They had come to say good-bye.

Here—under the full moon, on the spring equinox, a point in the year when day meets night—earth and sea would finally be separated, and for good this time.

Mom reached out from the carriage to throw her arms around me. "Oh, Emily." She sobbed, grasping my hair, pulling me to her so tightly I couldn't breathe. I didn't care. All that mattered was that I was in my mother's arms again. "I looked for you everywhere. Everyone on the island has been searching. We found every last jewel that Neptune had been after, but we couldn't find the most precious one of all. You."

Dad had slipped into the water while she was talking. A second later, his arms were around me too. Hovering in the water next to me, he reached out to wrap me in his arms. "My little 'un," he said, his voice raw and broken.

"Windsnap!" Neptune bellowed. All three of us looked up at him. He was pointing at Dad. "Come here," he said firmly.

Dad let go of me.

"No!" I lurched toward him, gripping him around the neck with my arms. This was it. Neptune could undo everything, put an even stronger curse on me if he wanted. My dad was going to be taken away; I'd say good-bye to him for the last time. "No! Please!" I begged.

Dad unpeeled my fingers from around his neck. "It'll be OK," he said, the quivering in his voice giving him away. He didn't believe that any more than I did. Then he looked at Mom. "I always loved you," he said. "And I always will, right?"

Mom swallowed hard and nodded.

Dad glanced at Neptune, who glared back at him. "I have to go," he said. Kissing Mom's hand, ruffling my hair, he turned and swam away.

I darted through the water to follow him. Gripping his arm, I swam alongside him. Dad tried to shake me off. "Please, little 'un, don't make this harder than it already is," he said.

"Don't go," I begged. I swam to Neptune's chariot with him. "Please!" I begged Neptune, choking on sobs. "Please don't make me have to lose my dad again. Please. Please don't make them have to part. I'll do anything. I'll be good. I'll never get into trouble again. *Please.*" I let go of Dad and wept openly. I had nothing left to say, nothing to ask, nothing to offer, nothing to look forward to.

"Stop your crying, child," said Neptune. "Listen to me." He turned to Dad, looking him harshly in the eyes. "Windsnap," he said, "do you love your wife?"

"More than anything," Dad said. He looked around for inspiration—and found it in the sky. "More than the moon itself."

Nodding briskly, Neptune asked, "And she feels the same way?"

Dad glanced across at Mom. "I hope so."

Mom held her hands to her chest. Wiping her cheeks with the back of her hand, she nodded vigorously. In that moment, I knew what I'd known all along, really. Of course they loved each other! Everyone argues, even Shona and I. Mom and Dad were never going to split up. I'd gotten it all out of proportion. My overactive imagination, and my silly worries—that's all it had ever been. I hugged myself, grinning with pleasure and relief.

Neptune was silent for a long time. He put his trident down on the seat in his chariot and held the rings in both hands. Juggling them in his palms, he looked back and forth between Mom and Dad. His powerful face looked different. The lines of anger streaking down each cheek seemed to have gone. His eyes looked rounder, softer. For the first time ever, I noticed how green they were.

In the darkness, rain began to fall, tiny, sharp droplets plopping onto the sea all around us. Neptune opened his mouth to speak again.

"No one has to say good-bye tonight," he said quietly. He turned to Mr. Beeston. "Beeston," he said, "you were wrong."

Mr. Beeston swam forward. Bowing so low his hair fell right into the water, he babbled, "Your Majesty, if I have failed you in any way, I——"

Neptune raised a hand to silence him. "You acted out of loyalty. But you are mistaken when you say I know what is important in life, what really matters. I don't at all. Or if I do, I have only just found out." He looked up at the mist, still swirling around the castle. The rain fell harder, bouncing off the sea all around us. "I have only just remembered."

Then he held the rings out in front of him. "Come here, Windsnap," he said. Picking up his trident, he nodded to the dolphins, who instantly swam forward, bringing the chariot and Mom to Neptune.

What was he doing? "I will no longer hide from the truth. I will no longer attempt to bury my feelings," he said.

Neptune called Aaron to him. "You are the man of the family now," he said to Aaron. "I cannot undo what has been done. But I can make amends.

You are free to travel, to live where you please, mix with whomever you like. I will not hide you from the world any longer. You are my fin and blood, and I am proud of you."

Aaron smiled hesitantly at Neptune. His eyes, his deep green eyes. Neptune's eyes.

"Your Majesty, sir," he said, "What about my mother?"

"She will be waiting for you at the castle."

"Is she . . . ?"

Neptune nodded. "She will be fine," he said. "Like you, she has a long life ahead of her. I want you both to enjoy it."

"You mean she's better? We're no longer cursed?" Aaron burst out.

Smiling, Neptune replied, "I will no longer allow curses. They are forbidden—by law!"

Aaron punched the air. Then he turned and smiled the widest smile at me.

Neptune turned back to my parents. "I am a firm ruler," he said, "and I always will be. No one can ever try to deny this." Mom and Dad both nodded, waiting for him to continue.

"But," Neptune went on, beckoning me to come to him, "this daughter of yours has brought something back to me that I lost many hundreds of years ago." He fell silent.

"The rings?" I asked, hoping to prompt him,

even though I should have known better than to interrupt Neptune.

"No," he said gently, "not the rings. You and your family may never fully understand what you have given me, but, let me tell you, it is the most valuable thing. In return, I give it back to you." Then he reached out to Mom and Dad—and handed them the rings. The diamond one to Dad, the pearl to Mom.

Silently receiving the rings, Mom and Dad gazed at each other, at me, at Neptune.

"You represent what I have lost, and you will represent its revival too." He spread his arms upward to the sky. "It is the spring equinox," he said, "the day of my wedding anniversary, the day of new beginnings. Merfolk and humans will from now on live in peace together. I order it!"

I gasped and looked at Shona. *Really? Did he really say that?*

"Not just on one small island. It's time for the whole world to start again. We will start a new world. A new world that is not a new world at all. The world that was there all along, to anyone who was not too blind to see it."

Then he turned back to us and frowned. "But you must make me a promise," he said sternly. I *knew* there'd be a catch. I knew it couldn't be that simple. Nothing in my life ever was.

"You must swear to me that these rings will never again be parted."

Dad grinned so widely that his smile almost broke his face in two. Grabbing Mom around the waist and pulling me toward him with his other arm, he replied, "Your Majesty, that is the easiest of promises to keep."

Neptune smiled. "Very well. I have said all I need to say." Holding his trident in the air, he waved it in the direction of *Fortuna*. A group of dolphins broke away and swam off toward it. "Your boat will be fixed by morning," Neptune said. "Now go. Travel the world. See new sights. Pass the message on to all you meet."

"We will," Mom breathed. "We won't let you down, Your Majesty. How can we ever thank you?"

Neptune waved her words away with his hand. "Just respect the rings and what they represent. I am giving you a great responsibility. You must show me you are ready for this. I shall be watching you."

With that, Neptune snapped his fingers and held his trident aloft. Motioning for Mr. Beeston to join him, he sat back down in his chariot.

"Look, I never meant you any harm," Mr. Beeston mumbled as he passed. Blushing and stammering, he added, "I didn't mean to—you know. I mean, it was just duty, you understand. Loyalty. I mean, Neptune. He's the king. We're still friends, aren't we?"

"Friends?" Mom spluttered. "When have we ever been real friends?"

Dad touched her gently on the arm. "Penny," he said, "it's a new world. We have to set an example."

Penny. He called her Penny! Things really were back to normal. Better than normal!

"Just like that?" asked Mom. "After everything?"

Dad nodded. "Look at all we have to be grateful for. Let's start again."

Mom turned to Mr. Beeston.

"Very well." Mom sighed. "We'll try. As long as you remember that you have to be loyal to us too now."

"I will," Mr. Beeston simpered. "I will. Thank you. Thank you." Then he gave me one last lopsided smile. "No hard feelings, eh?" he said, reaching out to ruffle my hair.

I stiffened, dodging his hand. "Mm," I said. I wasn't ready to forgive and forget yet.

"Emily," Dad said firmly.

"OK. Whatever."

And then the strangest thing happened. We looked at each other, me and Mr. Beeston. And for the first time in my life, I felt that we really saw each other—saw, heard, and understood each other. I saw someone like me. Desperate to fit in, to please, to belong. That was all he wanted underneath his creepy, sneaky ways. And when he smiled at me, I didn't recoil and squirm and think about his crooked teeth and his odd eyes. I found myself smiling back. "Yeah," I said. "No hard feelings."

"That's a good girl," he said.

"Beeston!" Neptune called again, and Mr. Beeston swam off to join him in his chariot. As the dolphins pulled them along, the moonlight lit a trail ahead of them.

In the silence of the night, I could hear Neptune's voice as they sailed away. "I forgive you," he called to the sky. "I forgive you, Aurora."

As his words echoed through the night, Dad pointed up into the sky. "Look at that," he said. I wouldn't have thought it possible if I hadn't seen it with my own eyes. The moonlight sparkled on the sea and lit up the raindrops that kept falling. In the distance, the castle stood dark and solid. But the mist had completely cleared. In its place, framing it with a perfect arc, every color bright and clear, was a rainbow.

"Just go through it once more," Millie said, blinking around at us all on the front deck. Aaron's mom was sitting on the front benches with her and Mom. She looked just like Aaron, thin and pale, with jet-black hair. She hadn't said much since she'd joined us, but she'd smiled a lot—a great wide smile that infected everyone around her, just like Aaron's now.

Dad leaned over a rail along the side of the boat. Aaron was in the water with me and Shona.

The sky was pale blue, wispy clouds floating lazily across it, each one tinged with pink edges. Millie had only just woken up. None of the rest of us had been asleep at all. How could we have slept on a night like this?

Mom laughed as she handed Millie a cup of tea. "We've told you the story three times now!"

"Yes, but I still don't believe it!" Millie replied, closing her eyes in ecstasy as she sipped her tea.

"Nor do we," Dad said, smiling at Mom as he reached for her hand. The rings shone on their fingers. "But it's true."

Millie took another gulp from her cup.

"We can go anywhere we like," Mom said. "We don't need to hide what we are." Then she glanced at Shona. "Of course, we'll go back to Allpoints Island first. These last few days I've realized how much everyone there cares about us." She smiled at me. "And I've realized a lot about what really matters to me. We may even stay there for good if we want to."

"Swishy!" Shona and I shouted in unison.

"Can we go too, Mother?" Aaron asked.

"I don't see why not," his mom replied with a laugh.

"Of course you're coming too," Mom said, linking her arm. "We're not letting you go that easily."

"And if we ever get bored with Allpoints Island, we'll move somewhere else. Anywhere we like," Dad said, his eyes shining with excitement.

"And if we don't, we'll just take lots of vacations." Mom smiled.

"We'll visit every country, every land, every sea," Dad went on. "We'll show the whole world they can get along in harmony like us!"

"We will, darling," Mom said, smiling back at him. "And maybe we'll even bring a tutor along with us so Emily doesn't miss out on school."

"Perfect!" Dad said. "She'll come back from her travels and still get top grades in Shipwrecks and Sand Dunes."

Mom's face tightened. "I was thinking more of math and spelling, Jake."

"I'll get her a new hairbrush, a whole set of hairbrushes, and an ocean chart so she can recognize all the fish in the sea."

"Or a ruler and a dictionary," Mom insisted.

"Oh, you two." Millie sighed. "You're not at it again, are you?"

Mom and Dad looked at each other and burst out laughing. "OK," Dad said. "Maybe changing the world is a bit ambitious just now."

"We'll start small," Mom said, reaching for his hand.

Dad kissed her palm. "Lead by example," he said. "No arguing."

"Never," Mom agreed.

"Come on," I said, "let's get going. Shona needs to get back to her parents!"

We'd hooked *Fortuna* up to some ropes so we could tow it back. I don't know what Neptune had done, but the lower deck was dry and sealed up so it floated like a normal boat. "We'll put it back to normal when we get home." Dad smiled.

With a bit of help from Aaron's maps, we'd set a course back to Allpoints Island. Dad reckoned it would take only a few days if we took turns pulling. He had left it to the three of us for now while he hitched onto the side of the boat near Mom.

Shona and Aaron and I pulled on the ropes as we set off, flipping our tails to make rainbows with the water, ducking under to see the rubbery round yellow fish with big black eyes bouncing on the seabed, racing and chasing each other.

As we passed the castle, we fell silent. Without the mist, it looked almost naked. Lonely, even. "We'll come back," Aaron's mother called down. "Even if it's just for a visit."

Aaron smiled up at her, then splashed me and grinned. He pulled his rope taut. "Race you to the next wave!" he said.

Shona dived down to follow him. But I stayed close to the boat for a while. The sky was growing lighter and lighter. Up behind me I could hear Mom and Dad talking.

"I've got nothing against rulers," Dad was saying. "But protractors? I mean, come on, does she really need one of those?"

"I tell you what," Mom replied. "I'll let you have the scale polish if you give me the algebra set."

"The scale polish and a kiss," Dad said.

"Done."

They were quiet for a while after that.

I smiled to myself as we swam on. What lay ahead for us? Where would we go? What would the future hold?

I couldn't answer the questions spinning around in my head any more than I could stop Mom and Dad from bickering about my schooling, or Shona from worrying about her hair, or Millie from trying to tell fortunes with coat hangers.

It didn't matter. What mattered was what I could see around me: my best friend racing our new friend along the waves; Mom and Dad smiling at each other and joking and kissing; Millie spreading the tarot cards out on the deck for Aaron's mom.

And beyond that? Well, beyond that lay a brand-new day.